DEATH STALKS YELLOWHORSE

DEATH STALKS YELLOWHORSE

Lewis B. Patten

Chivers Press • G.K. Hall & Co.
Bath, England   Thorndike, Maine USA

This Large Print edition is published by Chivers Press, England, and by G.K. Hall & Co., USA.

Published in 1997 in the U.K. by arrangement with Golden West Literary Agency.

Published in 1997 in the U.S. by arrangement with Golden West Literary Agency.

U.K. Hardcover ISBN 0–7451–8858–3 (Chivers Large Print)
U.K. Softcover ISBN 0–7451–8888–5 (Camden Large Print)
U.S. Softcover ISBN 0–7838–2006–2 (Nightingale Collection Edition)

Death Stalks Yellowhorse was first published by The New American Library.

The text of this Large Print edition is unabridged.
Other aspects of the book may vary from the original edition.

Set in 16 pt. New Times Roman.

Printed in Great Britain on acid-free paper.

British Library Cataloguing in Publication Data available

Library of Congress Cataloging-in-Publication Data

Patten, Lewis B.
    Death stalks Yellowhorse / by Lewis B. Patten.
        p. cm.
    ISBN 0–7838–2006–2 (lg. print : sc)
    1. Large type books.   I. Title.
[PS3566.A79D43   1997]
813′.54—dc20   96–44971

CHAPTER ONE

Hickory Marks was about an hour out of the town of Yellowhorse when it first caught his eye. He was half asleep, having ridden all night, and for a moment it didn't register. Then he sat up straight and turned his horse toward it. He knew what it was even from half a mile away. It was the body of a man and it didn't move.

He circled a little and came on it from upwind so that his horse wouldn't spook. He swung to the ground, stiff from being in the saddle so long. He recognized the body before he got to it. Dan Jerrold it was, and he was dead.

He wasn't a pretty sight. Hickory hadn't seen anything like what had been done to Jerrold since the war. He had been opened up from crotch to breastbone with a knife. He'd been crawling toward town. God only knew how long, trying to hold his insides in and not succeeding very well. He had died here, his face down in the dirt, one of his hands like a claw dug into the ground ahead of him.

Hickory looked back along the trail Jerrold had made as he dragged himself along. It was the kind of trail somebody would make dragging a sack of grain. There wasn't anything Hickory could do for him right away, except maybe to find out who had done this to him and why, so he went to his horse, mounted, and rode back along the trail Jerrold had made.

He scowled as he rode. This particularly bothered him because as far as he knew, Jerrold had been well liked. He ran the general store in town and the saloon next to it. To Hickory's knowledge he didn't have an enemy, and a killing like this one had to have been done because of a mighty powerful hate.

Hickory Marks was sheriff of Comanche County, Colorado Territory, and had been since Sheriff Banks was killed in a fall from a horse two years before. He'd been the sheriff's deputy before that and had taken over the sheriff's job when Banks was killed. When he ran for sheriff on election day, he was unopposed.

He was forty years old, born when Andy Jackson was President and named for him. He was lean and dark-skinned and there was gray in his hair and mustache. He did not consider himself handsome, but he carried, nevertheless, a certain male attractiveness that came, perhaps, from his own self-assurance and competence.

Comanche County was probably as thinly populated a county as there was in the Territory, and Yellowhorse, the county seat, had only thirty-seven permanent residents. But it wasn't small in area. It ran east and west for sixty miles and north and south for thirty at

2

one end, twenty at the other. It took a lot of riding for Hickory to get the business of the sheriff's office done.

Jerrold's trail was longer than he had thought it would be. It went up over a ridge and down on the other side and then down into a deep wash and out again. Then it went up over another ridge. Hickory thought of the agony Jerrold must have endured crawling that far in the shape he was in, and he made up his mind that he'd get whoever had done it if he could. He intended to find where it had happened, look around, and then go back and load Jerrold up and take him in to town. Then he'd start after the murderer.

From the top of the second ridge he could look down on the place where Jerrold must have been attacked. Jerrold's horse lay down there on his side, saddle and bridle still in place. Puzzled by that, Hickory rode down, kicking his horse into a lope.

Jerrold's horse had not been shot. His throat had been cut, clear through his windpipe. He'd bucked around some after it happened from the looks of the tracks and blood, but eventually loss of blood had weakened him and he'd just laid down and died.

Hickory was beginning to get a funny feeling in his spine. It wasn't exactly a chill but it was close to one. His stomach felt empty and he raised his eyes to scan the horizon all around. He didn't see anything so he got down off

3

his horse.

There were signs of a scuffle on the ground and in one place a big spot of dried blood. That was where Jerrold's trail began. But before starting to crawl Jerrold had scratched out two letters in the dirt. Wind had blown them some but they looked like an 'I' and an 'N.'

Why he'd stopped before finishing wasn't clear, but maybe his sense of urgency over what had been done to him had become overpowering. It didn't matter anyway. Hickory had already seen by the tracks on the ground that Jerrold's attacker had been wearing moccasins. The letters only confirmed what he already knew. An Indian had killed Dan Jerrold. And he'd done it in a way that had to make anybody's blood run cold.

The more Hickory Marks thought about it, the colder that little chill in his spine became, because he had a hunch he knew what this was all about. And if he was right, then it was trouble for the whole town of Yellowhorse.

He climbed on his horse and rode back to where he'd left Jerrold. He kept looking back and all around uneasily, as if somebody was after him.

About six months before, there had been a big Indian battle about a hundred miles north of Yellowhorse. A bunch of ragtag volunteers from the Territorial capital had jumped a Cheyenne Indian village and wiped it out. The people in Yellowhorse had felt edgy for a

4

couple of months after they heard about it but nothing happened and eventually they relaxed.

One of the volunteers who had been in the fight owned a rundown carnival that he had brought through Yellowhorse afterward. He only stayed a day and a half because all the people who were going to had by that time seen his carnival and paid the quarter he charged them to get in.

Hickory hadn't been in town when the carnival arrived. He'd been pursuing a horsethief who had got away. But he'd heard about it immediately when he got back. They had a couple of coyotes and a gray prairie wolf. There was a bobcat and a young mountain lion, some rattlesnakes made so sluggish by cold they wouldn't move, a Gila monster that wouldn't move either, and a badger that snarled at everybody that came close.

What was unusual about their exhibits was a couple of Cheyenne kids that the owner had taken prisoner after the fight up north. He'd had them in a cage like the animals, at least until Lila Anthony came storming in and took them away from him. There hadn't been a speck of heat inside the tent and the kids hadn't been dressed too warmly. They were coughing and sick, and maybe that was why the owner hadn't argued much with Lila Anthony.

The kids didn't hang on long. One died the next day and the second died the day afterward. Chris Dobbs made little coffins for them and they were buried up on the hill with William Whatley, the town's part-time preacher, saying Bible words over them for all that they were heathens and not Christian like the folks in town.

Now, Hickory Marks couldn't help concluding that one of the dead kids' relatives, likely their father, was here, but he couldn't begin to guess how much it was going to take to satisfy the Indian's thirst for revenge.

He rode back to where Jerrold's body was. Because of the way Jerrold had been mutilated, he couldn't load him as he ordinarily would. He had to wrap him in his blanket and tie it around and around with his rope from head to foot. Once that was done, Hickory lifted him and laid him across the saddle and then tied him in place. He mounted behind him and headed toward town.

He reached it in about an hour. Yellowhorse wasn't much of a town. Its one street was really just a wide place in the road running through. It was lined for about a hundred yards with buildings on both sides. There were some cabins and shacks scattered around, and three houses, one belonging to Jerrold, another to Chris Dobbs, who owned the livery stable, the third to Lila Anthony. Chris used part of the stable for a lumberyard and, being a good carpenter, also made furniture and coffins when there was a need.

Sheriff Marks turned in at the livery barn,

6

rode up the ramp, and slid off his horse just inside the door. He knew he'd been seen riding in, because, through the open door, he could see people gathering. He untied Jerrold and, with Chris Dobbs' help, eased him off the horse. Together they carried him into the part of the stable where Dobbs did his carpenter work. Dobbs asked, 'Who is he?'

'Dan Jerrold.'

Dobbs whistled. 'What happened to him?'

'Somebody killed him.'

'How?'

Hickory said, 'You'll find out anyhow, but for God's sake keep it to yourself. Somebody cut him open like a hog.'

Dobbs's face was white, his eyes shocked. 'Who the hell would do a thing like that?'

Hickory didn't answer because people came crowding in the door. He went out without answering any of their questions and headed for Jerrold's house. Jerrold had a wife and two kids and Hickory knew he ought to tell them before they got it second-hand.

All the way he kept trying to convince himself that there wasn't any connection between Jerrold's murder and the deaths of the two Indian kids. But he couldn't, because unless the kids were involved there just wasn't any reason why a lone Indian would kill Jerrold the way he had.

But it puzzled him how the Cheyenne had found out where the kids had died. He must have run down the owner of the carnival, Hickory thought. Maybe he'd known enough English to talk to the carnival man or maybe he'd had an interpreter along with him. One thing was certain, though. The carnival man would have told the Indian everything he knew. Indians had ways of getting what they wanted out of a man.

Jerrold had been the wealthiest man in Yellowhorse and his house showed it. It was big and square and had two stories like some of the houses in Denver. It was painted white and had a white picket fence around it and grass planted in the yard. There was a stained-glass window in the front door and a twist bell underneath. But Hickory didn't need to twist the bell. Mrs Jerrold had seen him coming, and she opened the door and came out on the porch as he climbed the steps. In the bright sunlight what had happened suddenly seemed impossible to him.

Mrs Jerrold, a plump, motherly woman said, 'Good afternoon, Mr Marks.'

He nodded as he took off his hat. He plunged right in, knowing that was the kindest way. He said, 'I got some bad news for you, ma'am. Mr Jerrold is dead.'

Her face went white and he thought she was going to fall. He took hold of her arm and helped her into the house. He eased her down into a chair. She said unbelievingly, 'How can that be? He was all right this morning.'

'Yes ma'am.'

'You've made a mistake. You must have made a mistake.'

'No ma'am. I knew Mr Jerrold. It was him all right.'

She stared straight ahead at nothing for a long time. Getting uneasy, he said, 'Mrs Jerrold?'

She looked blankly at him. 'Yes?'

'You all right, ma'am? You want me to send one of the other women over here?'

'What happened? Was it an accident? Was he thrown from his horse?'

Hickory had known that this would come, but he dreaded it. He said, 'No ma'am. He was killed.'

'Killed? By who?'

'I don't know yet. I'm going out now and get on the trail.'

She didn't answer him and he wondered where her sons were. One was seven and the other nine. He didn't want them to hear about their father from the other kids in town, so he said, 'Where are the boys, ma'am? Maybe you'd rather tell them yourself than to have them hear it from just anybody.'

She looked up. 'Yes. Thank you, Mr Marks. I'll call them in.'

He left, and before he reached his horse he heard her calling them. The town was so small her voice carried over all of it. They'd hear, and come, and she'd tell them about their pa.

He rode straight out of town. He glanced at the sun as he did, and decided he had maybe four or five hours before it would be too dark to trail. Not that he expected to find anything in that length of time. The Indian's trail would probably just wander around or, if he wanted it to, disappear.

But Hickory had a hunch the Indian wasn't going anyplace. He'd stay nearby, within a dozen miles, and wait for a chance to strike again. He wondered how the Indian had managed to get so close to Dan Jerrold. Plainly Dan hadn't suspected anything.

The Indian might be figuring on making him his next victim, Hickory thought, and wondered if he shouldn't go back to town and get a couple of men to ride with him. That would be the smart thing to do, but it would also give away the fact that the killer was an Indian, something Hickory didn't want getting out, at least not until he was sure his suspicions were correct.

He reached the place where Jerrold had been killed and right away took the Cheyenne's trail. The moccasin tracks led up over a hill and down. In the gully on the other side, he found where the Indian had left his horse. He must have seen Jerrold coming from a long ways off. He'd met him afoot, maybe pretending to be hurt. Jerrold's attempt to help had cost him his life. He'd have been better off killing the Indian like a coyote, but Jerrold hadn't been that

10

kind. Besides he hadn't been carrying a gun.

Like Hickory had figured, the trail didn't line out straight away from where the Indian had mounted his horse but wandered aimlessly and doubled back. Hickory had trailed for two hours when he suddenly realized he was looking down from a ridge at the place where Jerrold had been killed.

Once more he felt that cold chill running along his spine. The Indian had watched while he backtracked Jerrold to where he had been attacked. He'd watched while Hickory rode back, loaded Jerrold, and rode toward town with him.

Hickory knew, then, that his first suspicion had been right. This Indian was bent on vengeance for the deaths of those Indian kids. Vengeance against the whole town of Yellowhorse. And it was in Lila Anthony's house that they had died.

CHAPTER TWO

It was plain when Sheriff Marks got back to town that Chris Dobbs hadn't kept his mouth shut about the way Dan Jerrold died. There was a cluster of people in front of Jerrold's store and they all looked scared. Hickory figured there was no longer anything to be gained by being secretive, so he rode to them, dismounted, and tied his horse. After all, he thought, these people had helped elect him and he owed them the truth now that he knew it was the truth.

They fired half a dozen questions at him all at once. He said, 'Come on in the saloon. I'm tired and I want a beer. Then I'll talk to you.'

He went inside and crossed to the bar. Marsh Haggerty, his bald head like a bullet and his eyes close-set, asked, 'What'll it be, Hickory?' Haggerty tended bar for Jerrold and helped in the store when the saloon was closed or when things were slow.

Hickory said, 'Beer.' Outside, the sun was setting and the sky bright orange. It put a warm copper glow in the street.

Haggerty filled a schooner and slid it down the bar. He started taking orders from the men who had followed the sheriff in. Hickory drank half of the beer thirstily and put down the mug. He knew he was going to scare hell out of these men with what he had to say, but maybe knowing what they were up against would be no worse than trying to guess. He said, 'I trailed the Indian that killed Dan. The trail wandered around some, but it ended up right back where Dan was killed. That Indian was watching me when I found Dan and loaded him on my horse.'

William Whatley was the part-time preacher who had read the Bible over the Indian kids when they were buried. He was the town blacksmith weekdays and preached services every Sunday morning in the parlor of the boardinghouse. He asked, 'Why would he kill Dan? And why that way?'

Hickory said, 'The Cheyenne kids from the carnival. The ones we buried six months ago.'

Nobody said anything.

Hickory went on, 'The only thing I can figure is that this Indian is a relative of those two kids. Maybe he's their pa. He might have been hurt in the ruckus when they were taken prisoner. But he's all right now and he's come here looking for revenge.'

Len Cheever breathed unbelievingly, 'Why against all of us?'

Hickory shrugged. He could have said that during the day and a half the carnival had been in town and those two little kids were coughing and shivering in their cage nobody had protested or tried to get them out. Until Lila Anthony heard about it and came storming into the carnival tent.

Nobody spoke for a long time and Hickory could see that some of them were thinking just what he had been. Their eyes were guilty and they looked ashamed. But they were also scared. Finally Whatley said, 'You've got to stop him, Sheriff, before he kills any more of us.'

Hickory said, 'I'll try.'

'How are you going to do it?'

'I haven't figured it out. The only thing I

13

know is that there's no use trailing him. He'll just lead me on a wild goose chase. I'll have to think on it. He's not going anyplace. He's hanging around Yellowhorse, waiting for somebody to come out alone. I'd suggest you all try to be with somebody all the time. And carry guns.' He finished his beer. He was hungry now, and recalled that two days ago when he left town Lila Anthony had invited him for supper tonight.

He was suddenly anxious to get over there, maybe because he was hungry, maybe because he liked Lila, or maybe because of the chill that came into his spine whenever he thought of the Indian lurking around. He admitted that he was worried about Lila's safety. After all, the two kids had died in her house and that was information the Indian could have gotten out of the carnival owner along with the name and location of the town.

He went out and crossed the street. The sky had faded to a kind of pinkish gray.

Lila's house sat all by itself about a hundred yards beyond the livery barn. Hickory walked through the dry grass of the vacant lot. There was a pleasant smell in the air, of woodsmoke and cooking meat, of dust and dry grass and of the corral behind the livery barn.

Right away he could see that Lila and her son couldn't stay in their house tonight. Or any night until the Indian was caught or killed. The house sat all alone a hundred yards from

14

anything. She and Jess would have to come in and stay at the boardinghouse. So would Mrs Jerrold and her two boys.

Lila's house was small. It was the original building in Yellowhorse, built as a stagecoach way-station ten years before. It was constructed of hand-hewn logs that were graying now with age. It was stout enough, but it had windows that the Indian could go through.

Lamplight showed through the kitchen window. The sky was a uniform grayish color now. Hickory knocked on the back door and Lila opened it.

She was the kind of woman that made a man feel good just looking at her. A womanly woman, shaped the way she ought to be. Her throat was smooth and white, her mouth full and smiling, but her eyes held a worry that told him she had heard. She said, 'Come in, Hickory. I'm glad you remembered.' Lila did the cleaning at the boardinghouse. That it was menial work didn't bother her. A woman alone couldn't be picky about the way she earned her living as long as it was respectable.

She remained in his way without stepping aside so he grinned, took her face between his hands, and kissed her on the mouth. Kissing her always made him want more, but he was fifteen years older than she was and weathered and homely and he always told himself he ought to put those kind of thoughts out of his head. He was too blind to see that she wanted him and didn't care about the disparity in their ages. He thought she was just friendly and that those light kisses didn't mean anything.

He went around her, washed at the washstand, then sat down at the table. Young Jess was already there, watching him solemnly. He was four and he plainly liked Hickory Marks, but he was shy. Hickory mussed his hair, then looked across the room at his mother.

He thought her face was flushed from the heat of the stove, then remembered he hadn't noticed the flush when he came in. He wished that he wasn't so much older than she was even while he knew that was something that could not be changed.

She said, 'I heard,' with a glance at Jess.

Hickory nodded. She came to the table and began setting it. She smelled good and he wanted to put his arms around her and pull her down onto his lap. He didn't, and she finished and went away. Hickory asked, 'All of it?'

The color was gone from her face as she looked at him. 'All.'

He said, 'I figure it's got to be those two kids' pa. Or some other relative. Might be he was shot in the ruckus and laid up for a while. But now he's healed.'

'But why Mr Jerrold?'

'That redskin hates everybody in this town.'

Jess was watching his face as if trying to

16

understand all he was saying. He hadn't heard about what had happened to Jerrold and he couldn't piece things together without that knowledge. Which was just as well; there was no use getting him all worked up.

Lila took the lid from a dutch oven and lifted out the meat. She began to make gravy but Hickory could tell her mind was on the Indian. He said, 'You and Jess go over to the boardinghouse tonight.'

She swung around, her eyes now thoroughly scared. 'You don't think he'd come right into town?'

Hickory shrugged. 'Maybe not. But there's no use taking chances. They died here in your house. How's he to know you were trying to save their lives?'

She stared at him wordlessly, something of the sadness of that time and those two desperately ill children in her eyes. At last she nodded. 'All right.'

Hickory looked at Jess. 'You stay close to your ma the next few days.'

'Why?'

Hickory frowned, hesitating, but finally he said, 'Because she needs you.'

The boy started to question that, but when his mother put food on his plate he forgot what he had been going to say and began to eat. Hickory waited until Lila sat down, then took the platter from her and filled his plate.

Lila had been widowed for about four years. Her husband had been a stagecoach driver and had been killed over in the mountains when his stage went off the road and wrecked itself on the rocks below.

Most of the single men in town and on the surrounding ranches had courted her at one time or another. A few had been serious enough to ask her to marry them. She'd turned all of them down. She didn't intend to get married just for the sake of getting married. She had loved her first husband and had no intention of settling for less. She was self-supporting and content.

That was before she met Hickory Marks. She admitted that he wasn't the handsomest man in the world. She admitted that his calling was hazardous and would keep him away from home a good bit of the time. But there was something ... It made her tingle when they touched. It made her heart beat fast when she saw him coming through the grass toward her house. He was older; she admitted that. But it made no difference in the way she felt, even though it apparently made a lot of difference to him.

But, short of brazenly asking him to ask her to marry him, she didn't know what to do. She had tried all the subtle things women do to stimulate a man's interest. She had tried letting him know that she found him attractive. But, instead of treating her like a woman as she wanted him to, he persisted in treating her like a younger sister or a relative of whom he was very fond.

Now she watched him eat, a touch of exasperation in her eyes. She could go farther than she had, and knew it, but something in her rebelled at that. A man ought to want a woman as much as she wanted him. Otherwise it would be no good.

Her thoughts changed their thrust and turned to the Indian who today had killed Dan Jerrold in such a brutal way. She could not excuse it but she understood how the Indian must feel. The same way she would feel if Jess should be captured and put on display by the Indians, in a cold cage until he caught lung fever and died. She knew if that should happen she would feel just as vengeful and savage as the Indian did. She would be capable of things which, under other circumstances, would have been impossible.

It was dark outside when they finished. Hickory Marks wiped his mouth with his napkin, excused himself, and got to his feet. He stood there a moment, sombre eyes on the window, and then he said deliberately, 'Get your things together. Take your time. I'll be outside.'

He put on his hat, opened the door quickly, stepped out and as quickly closed it behind him, visible only for an instant to anyone outside. She stood there motionless for a time, listening for sound outside the house, hearing none. A small chill touched her. She scoffed at it but it did not go away.

She began picking up the dishes on the table. She poured water into the dishpan out of a teakettle heating on the stove and swished soap in it until there were suds. She put the dishes in.

In her mind she could see Hickory, standing motionless and invisible in the darkness beside the closed door. And she knew that if he wasn't out there she would be terrified.

Jess said, 'Ma, can I go outside and play?'

She shook her head. 'No. I want you to get the carpetbag out of the loft for me. We're going to stay at the boardinghouse tonight. Won't that be fun?' She didn't hear his reply. Her eyes were glued to the dark square of window and she could not take them away.

The Indian was out there someplace, watching, waiting. He would strike again. It would be unrealistic to expect even Hickory Marks to catch him before he had the chance.

Everything was against Hickory. The Indian had the upper hand. Unseen, like a shadow he lurked in the darkness waiting for one of the town's inhabitants to make a mistake.

When they did, he'd be ready and he'd strike. Hickory Marks couldn't be everywhere.

Jess climbed to the loft and handed down the carpetbag. Trying hard to keep her glance away from the window, she put into it the things that they would need.

Absently afterward she put away the dishes she had stacked neatly on the table after drying them. She tidied up the room.

There was a soft knock on the door and Hickory came in. His face was wary and still, his eyes narrowed against the light. Lila said, 'We're ready, Hickory.'

'All right.' He blew out the lamp and went back to the door. He went out first, turning then and saying, 'Hold onto your ma's hand now, Jess.'

The boy slipped his hand into hers. Hickory moved out ahead of them, both hands free, walking lightly like a cat.

The phrase from the Bible came to her mind. 'I will walk through the valley of the shadow of death and fear no evil. For thou art with me.' That was where she would be walking as long as the Indian lurked out there. But Hickory was with her and she was not afraid.

CHAPTER THREE

The grass, as they walked, made a rustling sound. The lights in the saloon and in the boardinghouse looked as if they were a mile away. Lila glanced fearfully to right and left, probing the shadows and dark places, seeing nothing.

21

The flesh on her back crawled. Half a dozen times in as many seconds she looked around. She realized that she was squeezing Jess's hand so hard she was hurting him. But he had not cried out.

Ahead of her, Hickory Marks walked, lightly, easily, more like an Indian in moccasins than a white man in boots. His head, too, swiveled back and forth as he tried to pick the most likely spot from which the Cheyenne would attack.

And she realized something she had not realized before. The Indian *would* attack. Hickory knew that and so did she. He was there in the darkness, his thirst for vengeance only partly satisfied.

Tense she was, as tense as a person under strain can get. Her hands were slippery with perspiration. Her skin crawled. Terror was like a bomb inside her head, a bomb that would explode at the slightest noise.

But it was no slight noise that split the air. It was a screech, seeming to come from the pits of hell. It froze the limbs and curdled the blood. It made the sweat that had dampened her body turn to ice. It rose and reached the pitch of a woman's scream, and wavered, and fell, and rose again.

Lila realized that she had stopped, probably the worst thing she could have done. Ahead of her, Hickory, gun in hand, had turned to face

22

the sound. But there was nothing to be seen. Only the same darkness that had been there before. Only the darkness out of which death would come.

It seemed that they stood there motionless for several minutes, but it could not have been more than an instant, part of a second at the most. Then Hickory snatched Jess up from the ground. He rammed his revolver back into the holster at his side. He seized her hand, his big hand swallowing her smaller one. She was yanked forward as he began to run, dragging her behind. He said, his voice hoarse and strange, 'Come on! If he had a gun, he'd a used it by now!'

She stumbled and nearly fell, but recovered and ran on. Hickory, with his size and bulk, was ponderous, but he wasn't slow. It was all she could do to keep up, but she had no chance to fall behind. His big hand pulled her on, forcing her, not giving her a chance to lag.

Once the screech had died out, the town was like a tomb. But even in the silence the Indian's cry seemed to echo and re-echo from the silent buildings, from the vast and silent plain.

Nor did the icy chill in Lila's spine go away. They reached the street, and plunged across, seeing the faces that had appeared in the windows of the boardinghouse, seeing the armed men that poured from the double doorway of the saloon.

Hickory neither slowed nor stopped until he

was inside the boardinghouse. Then he hauled up, released Lila, and put young Jess down on the floor. He said nothing, but the look he gave her could not conceal the relief he felt that she and Jess were safe. He plunged back out through the door, his heavy boots thundering briefly on the porch.

Lila wanted to hide, but she put down the carpetbag and forced herself to return to the door. Hickory was suddenly more important to her than her own life was. He was a rock, something to hold on to that would never change, never weaken, never go away. He made her feel safe and warm, and while her feelings told her he was indestructible, her intellect told her he was not.

From the saloon next door close to a dozen men had come. They had hesitated only briefly. All had guns. All felt the comfort that comes from numbers. While Hickory was still inside the boardinghouse, they had started across the street, bent over, running, guns held at the ready in front of them. By the time Hickory had turned and gone back outside, they were already across the street and in the grass-grown lot.

As Lila reached the door of the boardinghouse, crowding those already there and pushing her way out onto the darkened porch, Hickory roared at the men across the street, 'Come back here, damn it! You can't get him in the dark!'

A couple of the men looked around. One stopped, but when the others kept going, he went on too. Hickory raised his voice and roared again, 'Damn it, come back here!'

But the excitement of the hunt was on them, and with nearly a dozen of them, they felt invincible. They could eliminate the scourge, they thought, and they were not going to let the chance slip away.

But Hickory knew, if they did not, that they were playing into the Indian's hands. The dozen represented all but one or two of the men in town. They were leaving their families defenseless before an Indian who could move freely and unseen in the darkness, could strike and disappear and strike again.

Hickory was sure the Cheyenne had no gun. Otherwise he'd have used it a few moments before when he had screamed. Hickory also knew something else. Each of the dozen men going after the Indian had at least one gun. All the savage had to do was get one separated from the others and he'd not only have another victim, he'd have the victim's gun.

Hickory didn't think he could make the men return even if he went after them. But he couldn't stand here, do nothing and watch another man get killed.

Gun in hand, he ran across the street after the men, who had now disappeared. He bawled, 'Hey! Come back!'

It did no good. Glancing often to right and

left, he ran on after men he could no longer see. They had probably separated by now, he thought and they were more likely to kill each other than they were to kill the Indian.

Occasional gunshots boomed out ahead of him. And then Hickory stopped. If he came on them from the rear, he'd be the one to get shot. They wouldn't know but what he was the Indian.

Shrugging with disgust, he turned and headed back. Lila's house loomed to one side of him. He watched the shadows warily, trying to probe their depths, failing but still watching closely for movement and listening for sound.

Behind him the guns still cracked spasmodically. 'Damn fools,' he thought. Without incident he reached the street and started across.

He saw Lila's white face and Jess's scared one among the others on the porch of the boardinghouse. He didn't miss the expression on Lila's face. It made him feel warm inside.

He reached the boardinghouse porch and said, 'All of you had better get inside. The Indian had no gun before but he's probably got one now.'

They crowded each other in their haste. He waited until they all had disappeared, then went next door to the saloon. A couple of the town's older men were standing just outside the door looking apprehensively in the direction the others had gone. Marks said,

'Better get inside,' and they obeyed.

He put his back to the saloon wall, away from the light streaming from the windows. Gunshots still came spasmodically from the direction in which the group of men had gone. Hickory wondered how long it would take them to find out they couldn't get the Indian in the dark, that shooting blindly only wasted cartridges.

Suddenly, mingling with the shots, he heard a high yell of pain that ended as quickly as it had begun. After that there was a brief silence, then a redoubling of shots. Somebody had been hit, he thought sourly, which was just what he had expected. They'd come back now, carrying whoever had been hurt.

He waited, eyes straining to see into the darkness across the street. How do you combat a scourge like this Indian, he wondered. He couldn't be seen in the dark, and while he could be trailed by day, he could not be caught because he would always have several hours' start. The only way the townspeople could be sure that they were safe was if they stayed huddled together inside, and they couldn't do that forever.

The shapes of men materialized out of the darkness across the street. One, Juan Garcia, came running toward the sheriff. Out of breath, he panted, 'He got Len. Jesus, it was awful!'

Hickory asked, 'Is he dead?'

27

'I don't know,' Garcia panted. 'If he ain't, he oughta be. They're bringin' him.'

Hickory asked, 'What about his gun?'

Garcia stared at him unbelievingly. 'His gun? Is that all you care about? He's cut. He's bleedin' like a hog. And you want to know about his gun!'

Hickory said, 'No call to get riled. The Indian didn't have a gun. I'd just as soon it stayed that way.'

Garcia looked at him with a changed expression in his eyes. He said, 'I'm sorry. I didn't understand.'

More men straggled across the street. Then Hickory saw Marsh Haggerty and Max Kaminski coming together, supporting Len Cheever between them. They were half carrying, half dragging him. He showed no sign of life, but Hickory could hear him choking.

And he could see the blood. It had drenched Len Cheever's front, a scarlet mass. His head lolled helplessly to one side. Like Dan Jerrold's horse, his throat had been slashed by the Indian.

Kaminski and Haggerty reached the saloon and Hickory said, 'Take him inside. Keep him away from the boardinghouse. The women and kids are scared enough as it is.'

They took Cheever inside the saloon. Hickory followed and, when they laid Cheever on a table, picked up his wrist. He knew it was useless even as he did it. Len Cheever was dead. He had bled to death.

Straightening, he looked at the men who had carried Cheever here, at the others crowding in the door. He said, 'Make a count. Is everybody here?'

A couple of the men counted heads. Haggerty said, 'All here.' His bald head shone with sweat and his close-set, narrowed eyes were scared.

Hickory asked, 'What about Cheever's gun? I suppose the Indian's got it now.'

He saw the belated dismay that came to their faces as they realized what their ill-considered foray into the darkness had cost. The life of a man, and maybe more because now the Indian had a gun and could murder at will from cover of darkness.

Hickory had another unpleasant task to face. He had to tell Cheever's wife. It was doubtful if she had recognized her husband when they'd carried him across the street.

Before he went out, he raised his voice so that he could be heard by all the shocked men crowding the bar and clamoring for drinks. 'Don't go out unless you have to. If you do go out, get out of the light quick so he can't pick you off. Don't anybody even go to the outhouse alone.'

His warning quieted them and he went on out the door, stepping quickly to one side as he did, getting out of the light. He hurried next door to the boardinghouse. The door was closed and all the window shades had been drawn. He knocked and the door opened and he stepped quickly inside, closing it behind him. He said, 'Mrs Cheever?'

Her face told him she knew even before she came across the room toward him. He said, 'It's Len, ma'am. He's dead.'

She froze there in the middle of the room. Her face was white as ashes, her eyes wide with terror. Then, suddenly, her face contorted with weeping. Great sobs were torn from her. A couple of the other women came and put their arms around her and led her back through the boardinghouse parlor to a chair. Hickory couldn't see her anymore, but he could hear her sobs. Several children began to cry.

He saw Lila and beckoned her. When she was close he said softly, 'The Indian got Cheever's gun. Don't let anybody go outside. If you have to, tell them why.'

She nodded. He turned to go and she whispered, 'What are we going to do? Do we have to sit here like cattle waiting for him to slaughter us?'

Hickory shrugged. He had no answer for her. He had been trying to figure out a way to get the Indian but he hadn't had any success. Going out in a group after him in the darkness hadn't worked. Trying to run him down by daylight hadn't worked. But there had to be a way.

He said, 'I'll get Chris started making a couple of coffins. I'll get Len fixed up so his wife can look at him.'

Lila took his hand in both of hers and held it tightly for a moment or two. Then she released him and he went out the door.

For a couple of minutes he stood on the boardinghouse porch, staring into the darkness, looking for movement there. Then, running, knowing the Indian could be less than a dozen yards away, he headed for the saloon.

CHAPTER FOUR

The saloon was hushed as he burst inside. Several of the men were already getting drunk. Others stared emptily into space. Nobody was talking. The thoughts of every man in the place were on the Indian.

Hickory thought how incredible it was that a single man could so terrorize a town composed of three dozen souls. Incredible maybe, but it was happening.

Standing just inside the door, he said, 'Chris?'

Dobbs raised his head from the table where he had been resting it and stared at him, his eyes clouded with liquor. Hickory said, 'We need two coffins. How about going over and making them?'

Dobbs got to his feet. He looked scared at the thought of going out and Hickory said, 'A couple of men ought to go along with him. Anybody want to volunteer?'

There was an instant's silence. Nobody wanted to go. Then Max Kaminski growled reluctantly, 'I'll go,' and Juan Garcia said, 'Me too.'

All three got their guns and headed for the door. Hickory hoped nothing would happen to any of them on the way to the livery stable or after they arrived. If anything did happen, it would be hard to get anybody to go out afterward for anything.

But he couldn't let people huddle here in the saloon and next door in the boardinghouse indefinitely. The more they let fear control them, the less chance they'd have of getting the Indian before he killed them all.

At first, Hickory Marks had felt, if not sympathy, then at least understanding for the Cheyenne. Now he felt nothing but anger and outrage. After all, the people of Yellowhorse hadn't put the Indian children on display. They weren't responsible for the children's illness or for their deaths. Lila Anthony had rescued them and tried to save their lives, and it certainly wasn't her fault that she'd gotten them too late. If the Indian wanted vengeance, then the owner and employees of the carnival were the ones he should take it against. But he

32

probably already had, thought Hickory. Otherwise he wouldn't have known about Yellowhorse.

There was some grumbling at the bar and he looked that way. The men who had run out so recklessly after the Indian a while ago were drinking together, scowling at him and grumbling among themselves. Blaming him, he thought, for what had happened to Cheever. Blaming him because Cheever was dead.

Jim Erdman, who worked for Chris Dobbs at the livery barn called, 'Hey, Sheriff! Come over here!'

Hickory walked toward him. He nodded at Marsh Haggerty and accepted the beer Haggerty drew for him. He looked questioningly at Erdman. 'What's on your mind?'

'Why the hell ain't you doing anything? That sonofabitchin' Indian has killed two men. Ain't you supposed to keep things like that from happenin'?'

Marks felt his irritation rise. And he suddenly realized how edgy he had been since finding Jerrold murdered yesterday. He asked, 'What would you suggest?'

'Well, by God, for a starter you could've come with us a while ago. If you had, maybe Len wouldn't of got hisself killed.'

Hickory said, 'I did come after you, and I yelled at you to come back.'

'I didn't hear you.'

Hickory said, 'I came back after you began shooting at everything that moved. I figured you'd shoot me just as quick as you would the Indian.'

Somebody laughed but Erdman didn't smile. Instead, his eyes narrowed and his face grew flushed. He said, 'Maybe we ought to get ourselves a sheriff that ain't so goddam scared.'

Hickory felt his fists starting to clench. He made himself relax. He said, 'Maybe.' Then he grinned. 'But you ain't likely to find one here. Everybody here is just as scared as me.'

Erdman said, 'You makin' fun of me?'

Marks shook his head. 'No. But I don't intend to take any of your crap. I told you not to go out there, but you wouldn't listen to me. The result is that Len is dead and the Indian's got his gun. Which makes it just about five times as easy for him to kill the rest of us off.'

Olaf Cruthers, a horsetrader who supplied remounts to the cavalry at Fort Lyon said, 'Somethin's got to be done. We can't stay here forever.'

Marks said, 'We can stay in while it's dark. Daytimes we can go on just like before.'

'Jerrold was killed in broad daylight.'

'But Jerrold wasn't expecting anything. He had no reason to suspect he might be killed.'

Haggerty said, 'You want another beer?'

Hickory Marks nodded. He accepted the beer and shoved a dime at Haggerty in

34

payment for them both. The townspeople were feeling critical of him and he couldn't blame them much. He *was* supposed to keep the peace. It was his job to protect them from violence.

He thought about going out alone to face the Indian, but he immediately discarded the idea. The Indian's eyes were accustomed to the dark and his wouldn't be, at least not for a while. He'd be at a disadvantage and the Indian would strike instantly. Maybe later, he thought, if he couldn't think of anything else.

He finished his beer and went to the door. 'Anybody going to the boardinghouse?'

Several of the men indicated they were. They were the ones with families. Hickory said, 'Come on, then. Let's go.'

They assembled at the door, and when they were ready, Hickory said, 'Make it quick and stay together. I'll watch for the Indian.'

He went out ahead of them and stood beside the door studying the shadows up and down the street as the men streamed from the saloon and hurried to the boardinghouse next door.

He saw nothing and heard nothing, but he had the feeling that the Indian was there. Watching. Taking his time. He wouldn't attack a large group if he could help it. He'd wait, and try picking them off one at a time when they were alone.

He waited there in the shadows until all the men had disappeared into the boardinghouse.

Then he followed. He reached the boardinghouse without incident and climbed the three steps to the porch. He moved back into the shadows and stood there silently.

For an instant he was tempted to go ahead and play the game of cat-and-mouse with the Indian and get it over with, once and for all. He hated doing nothing and he knew getting rid of the Indian was his job. But he also knew it would be foolish. He'd be playing into the Indian's hands. He couldn't match the Indian's stealth. He'd lose, and be killed, and he couldn't even be sure of taking the Indian along with him.

He stayed in the shadows on the boardinghouse porch for twenty minutes. He could hear Dobbs sawing and hammering across the street at the livery barn. Finally, satisfied that he wasn't going to be able to spot the Indian, he went inside, quickly opening the door, as quickly closing it behind him.

The parlor was crowded with people. Most of the children had apparently gone to bed because he saw only a couple of the older ones. Lila Anthony was sitting on a sofa in the corner, Jess sleeping beside her, his head on her lap. Hickory crossed the room to her. 'Don't you have a room?'

She nodded. 'Yes. But I hated to wake him. And besides, I like the company. I guess I don't want to be alone.'

'The rooms are safe.' But even as he said it,

he was trying to remember whether there were any sheds or porch roofs the Indian could climb upon and thus enter the upstairs rooms. He recalled that there was a porch in back. There was also the one in front, which would give access to at least four rooms that faced the street.

Mrs Cheever came downstairs, apparently having been preparing the rooms upstairs for all the unexpected guests. Her eyes were still red but her face was composed. She was a big, bony woman, well liked by all the kids in town. She'd never had children of her own and she went out of her way to be good to other people's kids.

Hickory intercepted her. He said, 'I'd like to talk to you. Where the others can't hear.'

She nodded and led him to an unoccupied corner of the room. He said, 'The porches worry me. I'd like to put a man on guard in a room overlooking each of them. You'd know which rooms have the best view of the porches.'

She nodded, her eyes mirroring her fear.

Marks said, 'Put Olaf Cruthers and his family in one of them. Put Max Kaminski in the other one. I'll talk to them.'

He moved away. He caught Cruthers' eye and beckoned him. When Cruthers reached him, he said, 'The Indian could get into the rooms on the second floor by climbing onto the porch roofs. I'd like to ask you to stand guard in the back. If you get sleepy and want to be relieved, let me know.'

'I won't get sleepy. Not with that murderin' redskin loose out there.'

Hickory nodded. He left Cruthers, who got his family and headed for the stairs. He found Kaminski and his wife and told Kaminski he wanted him to stand guard in one of the second-floor front windows. Kaminski agreed.

Hickory returned to Lila Anthony. 'Want me to carry Jess upstairs?'

She nodded, giving him a weary smile. He gathered Jess up in his arms without waking him. Lila went to the stairs and Hickory followed her. She went to her room, unlocked the door, and went in. She started to light a lamp but Hickory said, 'Uh huh. Leave it dark.' He crossed the room and laid Jess on the bed after Lila had turned the covers back.

He turned. She was standing there, her face a white blur in the darkness. He said reassuringly, 'Don't worry. There's a man on guard front and back to be sure he doesn't try to get in by climbing onto one of the porch roofs. But lock your door after I go out.'

He kissed her lightly, finding her nose in the darkness instead of her mouth. She laughed nervously. He went out the door and waited until he heard her lock it behind him. Then he went back down the stairs.

William Whatley was pacing back and forth near the front door. He was a huge man, his upper arms as thick as an ordinary man's thighs. His neck was a column of strength and he had a full black beard. He intercepted Hickory and asked, 'What are we going to do?'

Hickory shrugged. 'I don't know. Have you got any ideas?'

'We could try and talk to him. When he finds out that it wasn't our fault that his children died in Yellowhorse...'

Hickory shook his head. 'You can't talk to him.'

'I'd be willing to try, if there was someone who could interpret.'

Hickory Marks shook his head. 'Uh huh. It would expose two men. And besides, it wouldn't do any good.'

'Then what do you intend to do?'

Hickory said, 'That Indian has killed two men, which makes him a murderer. If I can't capture him, I'll kill him. That's my job.'

'Wouldn't you do what he's doing if the same thing had happened to your kids?'

Hickory said, 'Mr Whatley, forgiveness and charity isn't what's called for here. That Indian wants to murder everybody in Yellowhorse. He'll do it if he can. Maybe I understand how he feels, but that's got nothing to do with it.'

'He's only one man. We ought to be able to capture him. We shouldn't have to kill him.'

Hickory said, 'I'd sooner try catchin' a grizzly bear.'

CHAPTER FIVE

Hickory Marks stepped out onto the veranda of the boardinghouse. The sound of Chris Dobbs's hammer across the street was peaceful and ordinary. In all the time Hickory had been sheriff, and in the time he'd been deputy, no one had been killed in Yellowhorse. Except accidentally. Now two men were dead, murdered, and the killer was still at large.

There was a chance, a good one, Hickory thought, that the Indian would get enough and disappear as suddenly as he had appeared. Nobody's thirst for vengeance could last through three dozen killings or even a fraction of that amount.

He took a cigar out of his vest pocket, bit off the end, and put it into his mouth. But he didn't light it. He just rolled it back and forth, savoring the taste.

He realized how tense and watchful he was. His eyes kept probing the shadows across the street. The hammering and the sawing continued at the livery barn.

The Indian might be gone for tonight, thought Hickory. Having sown his seeds of terror, he might very well have withdrawn. He might, even now, be riding a dozen miles away.

But because nobody knew, there'd be damn

little sleep for any of the townspeople tonight. And tomorrow, because they'd had no sleep, they'd be even more edgy, more irritable and quarrelsome than they had been tonight. They'd renew their demands that he catch or kill the Indian.

He got up suddenly, all indecision gone. He drew his gun and moved to the corner of the boardinghouse. Here, he froze, listening, letting his sharpened senses take in all the sights and sounds and smells of the town. Hell, he thought, the damn Indian was only a man. There was nothing supernatural about him. He could be killed like any man.

He stood frozen at the corner of the building for a full five minutes. Then he eased around it and walked carefully along the weed-grown passageway between it and the saloon. He stirred a tin can with his foot, froze briefly, and then went on.

The advantage the Indian had was his motionlessness. He could stand hidden and wait for his white enemies to come to him.

Knowing he was playing into the Indian's hands, Hickory nevertheless went on. Reaching the rear corner of the boardinghouse he stopped again and stood absolutely still.

Suddenly breaking clear of the building corner, he sprinted for the corner of the woodshed fifty feet away. He reached it and stopped, listening, trying to pierce the shadows with his glance.

41

Maybe, he thought, the Indian was across the street waiting for Dobbs and the men with him to come out. He felt himself relax slightly at the thought and knew even as he did that to relax was to invite death at the hands of the Indian.

He circled the shed, a careful step at a time, stopping often to listen. He heard nothing and started back toward the corner of the boardinghouse.

He sensed it rather than heard it. It was a whisper of sound, a movement of the air, a rustling of the grass, and he whirled. He saw the blur of movement and heard the whistling sound the gun made as, clubbed, it came rushing toward his head. He smelled the smoky odor of the Indian and raised an arm involuntarily to ward off the blow.

The gun barrel struck his upraised arm with enough force to turn it numb. But he had no time to wonder if the blow had broken it. The Cheyenne's body struck him, hard and powerful, and he knew that in an instant the Indian's knife would plunge itself into him. He had been a fool to come out alone and he'd known it, but he had done it anyway and now it was time to pay the bill.

The Indian had released the gun the instant that it struck. Hickory jammed his revolver against the Indian's body. He pulled the trigger but the Indian twisted away and the bullet tore into the wall of the boardinghouse. Hickory let the gun fall, knowing his time was gone. He grabbed for the Indian's hand, the one that held the knife.

Sharp steel bit into his hand, bringing pain and an instant rush of blood. He found the Indian's wrist and tried to hold it but failed because the blood made it slippery as a fish.

He was closer to death than ever before in his life. The knife slashed across his ribs, stopped only by the ribs themselves, and he groped desperately for it with his other hand. Missing it, he did the only thing left to him. He brought up his knee into the Indian's groin with all the force his desperation could give to it.

The knife, which had been poised to plunge itself into his heart, only raked his chest. The Indian fell away. He snatched up his rifle and ran away, bent over, obviously in pain. He disappeared into the darkness.

Hickory grunted, half with pain, half with disgust, as he stooped and retrieved his gun. He went around the corner and hurried to the front of the boardinghouse.

He was bleeding badly and his arm was numb, but he was lucky to be alive. What humiliated him was the knowledge that the Indian was unhurt. He had a bellyache from being kneed in the groin, but he'd get over that in an hour. Hickory would be stiff and sore, his fighting ability impaired for days.

He went into the boardinghouse, trailing blood along the floor. Mrs Cheever saw him

43

and immediately made him sit down in the nearest chair. She hurried away for bandages and was back in less than a minute, bandages in one hand, a bottle of whisky in the other.

Hickory sat slumped in the chair, his arms dangling. He could hear the steady drip drip of blood onto the floor. His arm ached ferociously and he wondered if the blow had broken it.

Mrs Cheever was efficient and she was fast. She had his wounds bandaged in ten minutes. Fortunately the cut on his hand wasn't deep. It was only painful. Glumly he assessed the damages. His right hand was hurt. His left arm was numb, even if the blow hadn't broken it. His body was bandaged and it hurt to move.

He had come off second best but at least they couldn't say he hadn't tried. He took a long pull on the bottle, then laid back and closed his eyes. His head whirled for a long time but at last he fell asleep.

He did not sleep long. The pain in his arm woke him and he sat up straight in the chair.

The boardinghouse parlor was deserted except for Mrs Cheever, dozing in another chair. From across the street, he could hear the sound of hammering. Uneasy, he got up.

Only one lamp burned in the boardinghouse parlor and it had been turned down low. Hickory withdrew his revolver from its holster, cocked it and released the hammer carefully. He had wanted to know if his cut hand would be able to hold it and he was relieved to discover that it was. Holding it hurt, but the bandages didn't impair his efficiency.

His left arm was something else. It ached ferociously and once more he wondered if the blow from the Indian's rifle had broken it.

He crossed the parlor to the front door and stepped outside. He stood motionless beside the door, staring into the darkness, listening for sounds.

Over his head, the porch roof creaked. He didn't wait and he didn't take time wondering what it was. He knew. He leaped forward, crossed the veranda, and ran recklessly out into the street.

His flesh was crawling because he knew if the creaking had not been caused by the Indian he was exposing himself to another savage attack. He reached the middle of the street and whirled, gun in hand.

A glance told him he had made no mistake. The Indian was on the roof. He was standing in front of one of the windows.

Even as Hickory raised his gun, a tongue of flame shot from the window at the end of the porch. Kaminski, he thought, and sighted his own gun on the now swiftly moving shape of the Indian. He couldn't see his sights and could only point the weapon. He waited until the Indian reached the end of the porch then fired, and fired again, knowing instantly that he had missed both times. But he hadn't wanted to shoot while there was a chance of his bullets going through the flimsy walls and hitting somebody asleep inside.

The Indian was gone, having leaped off the roof and vanished into the darkness.

Kaminski called down, 'I missed the sonofabitch. Did you hit him?'

'Uh huh. Missed him clean both times.'

Kaminski said, 'Trouble was, I couldn't see my sights.'

Hickory went back to the door of the boardinghouse. He went in, closing the door behind him. People were coming down the stairs, some of them dressed, some in nightclothes. All were scared. Hickory said, 'He was on the porch roof in front. Max shot at him and so did I, but we both missed. You can go back to bed.'

Mrs Spence said, 'Bed? Up there? Not me!' She took her two children and led them to a sofa against the wall where she settled down with one on each side of her like a hen with chicks.

Lila Anthony and Jess stood halfway down the stairs. Lila's glance met Hickory's. He could tell she had seen the blood on his shirt and the bandage on his hand. She came hurrying down the stairs, with Jess following.

There was deep concern for him in her eyes, and seeing it there made him feel warm. She said, 'You're hurt!'

'I tangled with that Indian a while ago.'

'And you didn't let me know?'

'You were asleep. Mrs Cheever fixed me up.'

'Did you go out after him all by yourself?'

He nodded, feeling a little foolish.

'You ought to know better, Hickory Marks!'

He grinned. 'Yes ma'am.'

'Don't you "yes ma'am" me! What happened just now? Was he on the roof?'

He nodded. 'Good thing I put Kaminski on guard up there. I just happened to hear him, but both of us missed him clean.'

Her face was white and her eyes frightened. She was thinking that it could have been her room the Indian was trying to get into. She stared at the two cuts in his blood-stained shirt through which the bandages were visible. She asked, 'Did he hurt you very bad?'

Hickory shook his head, thinking that if the Indian's knife had slashed two inches lower he'd have been opened up like Jerrold had been.

Lila said, 'This is a nightmare. I can't believe it's really happening.'

'It's happening. But staying awake isn't going to help. Go settle down on one of the sofas and see if you can't get some sleep.'

'Only if you'll promise not to do anything foolish again.'

He nodded. 'I promise.' He had no intention of trying to tangle with the Indian again. He'd barely gotten away with his life the first time and he'd been whole and unhurt. As stiff and sore as he was now, he wouldn't have a chance.

Lila studied him worriedly for a moment more. 'You're sure that you're all right?'

He nodded. He glanced down at Jess. The boy was half asleep. He still didn't seem to fully comprehend what was going on, which was just as well. Lila turned and led the boy across the room and Hickory settled down in a chair facing the door. If the Indian had tried getting into one of the upstairs bedrooms it wasn't inconceivable that he'd try coming in here.

Sprawled out and as comfortable as he could get with two slashes on his body, a cut hand, and a numb left arm, Hickory stared moodily at the door and wondered how long this was going to go on.

CHAPTER SIX

Hickory closed his eyes and tried determinedly to go to sleep. For a long time he was wide awake. What was happening had a nightmarish quality that made it difficult to believe.

He could hear the monotonous pounding of Chris Dobbs's hammer across the street. And finally, worn out, he dozed off.

He awoke with a start, wondering what it was that had wakened him. His ribs and his chest burned like fire. His arm still ached and

48

now his hand did too.

Then he realized it was the utter silence that had awakened him. The noise of Chris Dobbs's hammer had stopped.

Alarmed, he jumped to his feet. His rifle leaned against the wall beside the door and he snatched it up. His right hand, the one that had been cut, was stiff, but not so stiff he couldn't pull a trigger or shove a cartridge into the breech. He cocked the gun as he went out.

The street was empty, as far as he could see. There was a crescent moon hanging over the lower end of it, and while it left shadows, it illuminated most of the street.

Hickory heard voices from the direction of the livery barn, and felt himself relax with relief. Dobbs and those with him were apparently all right. Dobbs had simply finished with the two coffins and the three men were returning to the boardinghouse.

He saw them come from the wide stable doors and saw them start across the street. Two of them were carrying the coffins, bulky and stacked one upon the other, but light enough for easy carrying. The other came behind, probably serving as a guard.

They reached the middle of the street. Maybe the Indian had gone, thought Hickory. Then, so suddenly that he jumped, flame lanced from the muzzle of a gun in the shadows beside the livery barn. Hickory didn't wait to see if the bullet hit anything. He threw his own rifle to his shoulder and fired almost instantly at the muzzle flash. He flipped open the action and shoved another cartridge in, cocked the gun, and raised it a second time.

The two carrying the coffins had dropped them the instant the report of the Indian's gun shattered the silence in the street. The coffins made racket enough to wake the dead as they fell. The men who had been carrying them and the third, serving as guard, all sprinted for the safety of the boardinghouse.

Hickory held his fire, rifle raised, waiting for another muzzle flash at which to shoot. This time there would be no delay and he'd get the Indian, but he was disappointed. No muzzle flash came from the corner of the stable. There was only silence save for the heavy breathing of the coffin carryers and their guard, save for the pound of their boots on the veranda of the boardinghouse.

Chris Dobbs said exultantly, 'You got him! Come on, let's go take a look!'

Hickory said, 'Stay where you are. I never touched him. You go over there and he'll cut you to bits.'

'You think he's still there?'

Hickory wanted the Indian. He wanted another chance at him. But he needed a muzzle flash at which to shoot. Deliberately he lied, 'Uh huh. He's gone. Go on out there and get those two coffins and put 'em here on the porch.'

The men hesitated, but only briefly. Then, taking Hickory's word that the Indian was gone, they went hurriedly out into the street, put one coffin upon the other, and brought both back to the boardinghouse. Hickory stood with his rifle raised to his shoulder while they did, ready to fire the instant the Indian's gun flashed, but nothing happened. The men reached the boardinghouse and put the coffins down on the porch against the wall.

Hickory could hear voices inside the boardinghouse and over at the saloon. A lamp was lighted in the saloon and a man peered timidly out the door. 'What's going on?'

Hickory called, 'Nothing. Go on back to sleep.'

'What happened?'

'The Indian shot at the men carrying the coffins across the street. But he's gone now. Go on back to bed.'

He turned to follow Dobbs and the other two into the boardinghouse. He stopped when something in the direction of the Jerrold house caught his eye. He stood for a moment, watching it, then went on into the boardinghouse, cursing angrily beneath his breath. The goddamned Indian wasn't going to miss a thing. He'd not only murdered Jerrold and made his death slow and incredibly painful, but now he had set fire to Jerrold's house.

He went inside the parlor of the

51

boardinghouse. The shots had brought everybody downstairs. They stood around now, looking toward him, some in nightclothes, some fully dressed.

Hickory glanced around. The glow had grown strong enough to show red through the window curtains behind the drawn shades. Somebody said, 'Something's on fire! Something's burning!'

Hickory nodded. He said, 'Jerrold's house. That Indian ain't missing a trick.'

Mrs Jerrold cried, 'Oh dear God! No! Not the house too!' She ran toward the front door and Hickory, hating himself because he had to do it, caught her and held her before she got to it.

She was weeping now, hysterically. Lila Anthony quickly crossed the room and took Mrs Jerrold away from Hickory. Mrs Jerrold didn't fight. Instead she faced the people gathered there. 'Won't somebody help? We can save it if we hurry. Please! For the love of God, please help!'

William Whatley stepped forward. 'I'll help! Come on, all you men. Get buckets and blankets and come on!'

Several of the men headed toward the door. Hickory said, 'Hold on now! Nobody's going anywhere!'

Whatley's voice was shrill and full of outrage. 'What do you mean? We can save that house if we hurry. The least we can do is save some of her valuables.'

Hickory said inflexibly, 'No. That's what the Indian wants. Why do you think he set that blaze? He wants us to come out and fight it. Then he can pick off a couple more of us.'

'We can't stand here and watch it burn.'

Hickory asked, 'What's better, losing the house or losing a couple more of you? The Indian has a gun, but he doesn't need it. His knife is good enough.'

He had deliberately thrown in mention of the knife because everybody feared a knife vastly more than they feared a gun.

Mrs Jerrold continued to cry. She pulled aside the shade in one of the front windows and stood there, watching the glow increasing in the sky.

The fire grew rapidly. Ten minutes after Hickory Marks had first seen the blaze, it had turned the town almost as light as day. Flames shot a hundred feet into the air.

Hickory imagined the Indian, watching with glee the destruction of this white man's house. His own village had been attacked. Those of its inhabitants who could not escape had been slaughtered by the volunteers. His children had been captured. And afterward, everything burnable had been placed upon a pile and set ablaze including tipis, food supplies, clothing, robes, and everything else the soldiers didn't want for themselves. When it was over nothing had been left but blackened ashes and the snow and cold.

Once more Hickory couldn't help a feeling of sympathy for the Indian because he knew that had he been in the Indian's place he would have felt the same. He went to the window and as gently as possible pulled Mrs Jerrold away from it. The fire was dying now, a little. There was a blank expression on Mrs Jerrold's face. Her two little boys stood just behind her, faces white, eyes scared. Hickory said, 'Mrs Jerrold, I know it's hard. But you still have your boys and they need you now.'

She glanced up at him as if she had completely forgotten her sons. Then she turned, and knelt, and gathered them into her arms. They began to cry and, as she held them close, so did she.

Hickory raised his glance. There was hardly a dry eye in the room.

Lila Anthony and Jess were watching him. Tears were running across Lila's cheeks. Jess stood close beside her, looking scared.

Hickory went across the parlor and along the hallway that led to the kitchen. The kitchen was dark at this hour, but he had no trouble finding the back door. He opened it as silently as he could and stepped outside.

His stomach felt like a big hollow place. He admitted that his last encounter with the Cheyenne had scared the hell out of him. He was afraid to go out and face the Indian again, but there was a chance the Indian was across the street, watching the front door of the boardinghouse.

Angry at himself for his own fear, he pulled the door closed behind him. He stood there silently for a moment, rifle held in both his hands. Then, moving very quickly but still trying to be quiet, he rounded the boardinghouse into the narrow passageway between it and the saloon.

He had never given much consideration to his own courage or lack of it. He'd gone through the war and had been in his share of the battles and he'd been scared plenty of times. But he'd always done what he had to do and he'd never turned and run.

Now, alone in the darkness, facing an alien enemy who had hurt him so badly in their first encounter, he was suddenly more scared than he had ever been before. He wanted to turn around and run for the boardinghouse door. He wanted to get inside and lock the door and not come out again until daylight.

He was no match for the Indian and he admitted it. The man seemed as much at home in the darkness as a cat and he was incredibly savage and merciless.

But Hickory didn't stop. He'd overcome fear before and he would overcome it now. He went on, and reached the corner of the boardinghouse, where he stopped before letting the orange light from the burning house illuminate him.

Silent, motionless, he probed the shadows across the street, looking for the Indian. He knew the man was there, knew he had set the fire to draw the people out so that he could kill again.

He heard a rustle in the weeds behind him and whirled, ready to fire or, if the Indian was too close, ready to use the rifle as a club. He tightened his finger on the trigger preparatory to firing.

But it wasn't the Indian coming along the wall of the boardinghouse. It was Lila Anthony, and she had another rifle in her hands.

Hickory whispered, 'What the hell do you think you're doing here?'

'You've got no business coming out here alone! You're in no shape to fight him on equal terms. You're hurt!'

Exasperation was strong in him, and fear for her safety, but he was also pleased. She had cared enough to risk her own life. Her fear must have been greater than his but she had overcome it and had come anyway. He said, 'He's not over there anyway. Let's go back.'

She didn't argue or protest. She turned and headed back in the direction from which she had come. Hickory followed, worse scared now than he had been before but not for himself. If anything happened to Lila...

They reached the back corner of the boardinghouse without incident. After the fire glow in the street, it seemed unusually dark back here. Hickory positioned himself so that Lila was between him and the wall of the boardinghouse as they turned the corner and headed for the door.

He had the feeling that the Indian knew they were here, that he was only half a dozen yards away. He had the feeling they were going to be attacked.

He suddenly forgot the wounds made by the Indian's knife. They reached the back door and Lila opened it. He shoved her unceremoniously inside and backed in himself, still not quite believing that the Indian had not attacked.

He made it inside, closed and locked the door behind. The Indian could have entered the kitchen while they were gone. He could be waiting for them now. But Hickory didn't think so. He'd have felt it if the Indian had been here.

He turned and bumped into Lila and suddenly his relief that she was safe was so overwhelming that he forgot everything but the fact that she was close and that they were alone.

He leaned his rifle against the wall. He seized her and pulled her close to him and he lowered his head and kissed her on the mouth, bruisingly, hungrily.

Her response was startling. And suddenly he knew what she had been wanting him to realize all these months. He was not too old for her. It was enough that she needed him and he needed her. But there was more than that. Outside, a few minutes ago, he had known the fierce protectiveness of a man toward the woman he loves. He would sooner have died himself than have seen her hurt. Shaken, he pulled away. He said, 'Well, I'll be damned! What do you think about that?'

He knew she was smiling as she replied, 'I think that it is about time.'

CHAPTER SEVEN

Hickory Marks watched Lila Anthony and Jess climb the stairs to their room on the second floor. Then, weary beyond belief, he found himself a sofa and laid down, facing the door, his rifle on the floor close to his hand.

Loss of blood and pain had taken its toll. He still hurt where the Indian's knife had raked his body, and his hand still ached beneath the bandages, but the instant he closed his eyes he was asleep.

It was a dreamless sleep despite the Indian lurking outside. He awoke once during the night, cramped and hurting, but as soon as he changed position he fell asleep again.

Dawn woke him finally, seeping in at the edges of the window shades. The first thing he felt was a profound sense of relief. No more houses had been burned. No more people had been killed.

He got up, stretched, then picked up his rifle and headed for the kitchen. He could smell coffee and found Mrs Cheever there. Her face was drawn, her eyes red from weeping and sleeplessness.

He took a cup of coffee from her. While he sipped it, he studied her face out of the corner of his eye. She seemed to be numb with grief. He finished the coffee and went out the back door.

There was nothing fearsome about the town today and he felt instinctively that the Indian was gone. The Indian wouldn't wait around and risk being run down by the light of day. He'd have left several hours ago. Hickory knew that if he circled the town he would find the Indian trail leaving town. He also knew the Indian would be back tonight.

He went to the outhouse, then, on the way back, washed at the pump in the back yard of the boardinghouse. His own living quarters adjoined the jail down at the lower end of the street. He went there, shaved in cold water, and put on a clean shirt to replace the cut and bloody one.

For the briefest moment he let himself hope that the Indian would be satisfied with 'an eye for an eye, a tooth for a tooth.' The Indian had lost his two children. He had killed two of the town's inhabitants. His tipi had been burned by the volunteers. In retaliation he had burned Dan Jerrold's house. Maybe he was satisfied. Maybe he would not come back.

Hickory wanted to believe it but he could not. The way Jerrold and Cheever had been killed told him the Indian's burning thirst for vengeance would be far from satisfied.

He went back into the boardinghouse. The shades had been raised in the parlor and the front door opened. Lila Anthony and Jess were there. So were a number of the town's other inhabitants, including William Whatley. He intercepted Hickory and said, 'We should hold burial services today.'

Hickory nodded. 'I'll see if I can find a couple of men to dig the graves.'

Lila came to him, her face concerned. 'How do you feel?'

He grinned at her, holding her glance until she flushed. He said, 'Better.'

'Can we go out? There are some things I need at home.'

'Sure. I'll go with you.'

He followed her and Jess outside. Jess put his hand in Hickory's and tried to match his small strides to Hickory's longer ones. They crossed the street and cut through the grass along the path that had been worn in it.

Hickory took a cigar from his pocket when they reached Lila's house. He hunkered down against the wall in the bright sunlight and lighted it. He knew what Lila was doing inside the house. She was gathering up her keepsakes and valuables to take to the boardinghouse. She had faced the likelihood that her house also would be burned before this was over and she wanted to save the things she treasured most.

Jess came out and hunkered down beside Hickory, imitating him. Hickory wondered what you talk to a small boy about. He'd never been around children and while he liked them and they seemed to like him, he'd never been able to talk to them. But he'd learn. He grinned faintly. He'd learn.

Lila came out, carrying a worn carpetbag. He got up and took it from her and they walked back toward the boardinghouse. It seemed like a pitiful little to try and save from a house filled with the things people accumulate.

There were several men outside the saloon when he reached the door of the boardinghouse. Lila took the carpetbag from him and carried it inside. Hickory walked next door to the saloon. He said, 'I need a couple of men to dig graves for Dan Jerrold and Len Cheever.'

Max Kaminski said, 'I'll dig one.'

Olaf Cruthers, big and yellow-haired said, 'I'll dig the other one.'

Hickory nodded. 'All right. Go on up and start. As soon as you get done, let me know.'

The saloon was open and Marsh Haggerty

was already dispensing drinks. It was early but Hickory didn't say anything. After last night the men probably needed drinks as much as they needed food.

He went back to the boardinghouse. William Whatley was in the parlor and Hickory said, 'Kaminski and Cruthers are digging graves. They ought to be ready in a couple of hours.'

'I'll plan the services for eleven o'clock.'

Hickory nodded. Cheever's body was still over at the saloon, covered with a blanket and lying on one of the poker tables. Jerrold's was at the livery barn. The coffins were still on the boardinghouse veranda where they had been so hurriedly dumped last night. Hickory got a couple of men to take one of them inside the saloon and put Len Cheever's body into it. He had them take the other across the street.

Chris Dobbs was in his woodworking shop. He looked at Hickory as he came in. 'Think I ought to make some more?'

Hickory shook his head. 'Maybe we won't need them. Besides, the noise would upset people. They'd know what you were doing.' He paused a moment, then said, 'Hitch up a wagon. Put the coffins in. Whatley's going to preach the services at eleven o'clock.'

Dobbs walked back to the corral and caught two horses. He led them into the stable and while he harnessed one, Hickory harnessed the other. Each man backed a horse into place in front of a parked spring wagon and hitched him up. With that done, they carried Jerrold's coffin out and loaded it. Dobbs climbed to the seat and Hickory jumped up onto the tailgate. Dobbs drove out and across the street to the saloon.

Four men got Cheever's coffin from inside the saloon and loaded it. Hickory looked at his watch. It was still only a little after nine o'clock.

He was hungry, so he went into the boardinghouse. Usually Mrs Cheever only served meals at regular hours but this morning she was serving people as they came, since there wasn't room for the whole town to sit in the boardinghouse dining room. Hickory sat down at the table next to Whatley and his wife. He helped himself to scrambled eggs, side meat, and biscuits. He filled his coffee cup from the pot.

He discovered that he was ravenous. Whatley frowned slightly at him as if it was unseemly to enjoy food when two men lay dead, but Hickory paid no attention to him. Whatley and his wife finished before he did and left. Hickory sat there sipping his coffee, glad to be motionless.

How in the hell, he wondered, were they going to stop the Cheyenne? No white man could match his stealth. No white man was his equal in hand to hand combat, Hickory had found that out. The only solution Hickory

63

could think of was to get a troop of cavalry and surround the town with guards. And by the time a troop of cavalry could get here from Fort Lyon, half the people in town would already be dead.

He fished a cigar from his pocket, clipped off the end with his knife, and lighted it. He leaned back in his chair.

He heard the murmur of talk in the door. Half a dozen men were standing there looking at him. They seemed ill-at-ease, but their faces were determined. Chris Dobbs, apparently their spokesman, stepped forward and said, 'We want to talk to you.'

'Sure. Sit down.'

They came into the room and sat down across the table facing him. Hickory waited and finally Dobbs said, 'We think you ought to be doing something about that Indian.'

Hickory nodded. 'So do I. But I'm damned if I know what to do. Anybody got any ideas?'

Dobbs said, 'You're the sheriff. You're supposed to know what to do.'

Hickory said, 'I tried tracking him. It's a wild goose chase. He leads me away and then comes back. I tried going after him alone and he damn near killed me with his knife. You tried going after him in a group and he killed Len and got his gun.'

Dobbs said, 'Everything I've got is in that livery barn and in my house. Tonight he's going to burn one or the other unless he's stopped. By God, I want you to do something. I don't care what it is, but you been drawing sheriff's pay for years and it's time you started earning it.'

The other men grumbled their agreement with what Dobbs had said. Hickory suppressed his anger. He understood how they felt. He would have liked to lay it on somebody else himself, but there wasn't anybody else. It *was* his job to protect the people of Yellowhorse. And he hadn't been doing it. He said, 'Boys, I'll do my damnedest to think of something before it gets dark.'

The men, including Dobbs, nodded grudgingly. They sat there for several moments more, wanting to say more but not knowing what to say. At last they got up and filed silently out of the room.

Lila came in as soon as they had left. She sat down and said, 'I heard.'

Hickory said, 'I don't blame them. It *is* my job to do something about the Indian.'

'What can you do that you haven't done?'

He shrugged. 'I don't know. But there's got to be something. There's *got* to be!'

There was fear in her eyes. 'You're not going out after him again alone?'

Hickory shook his head. 'If I couldn't handle him before I was hurt, I wouldn't have much chance of doing it now.'

Whatley stuck his head inside the door. 'The graves are finished. We're going to have the services.'

Lila left to find Jess. Hickory went out into the street.

Dobbs had driven the wagon into the passageway between the saloon and the boardinghouse. The townspeople had formed a group behind it. Mrs Jerrold and her two sons walked beside Mrs Cheever directly behind the wagon. Both women were weeping and the boys looked scared. William Whatley followed them. Hickory walked behind the group that followed Whatley and after a moment Lila Anthony and Jess caught up with him. The spring wagon with the two coffins climbed the little rise behind the boardinghouse to the cemetery.

There were nine graves in the cemetery and two more that had been dug today. The newest of the markers were the wooden crosses that had been erected for the two Indian children who had died last winter. Nobody looked at them. It was as if they did not exist.

But Hickory looked. Burned in each cross were the words, 'Indian child, name unknown.' And that was all.

Two dead Indian children that the town had not even helped to kill. And because of them two more were dead, a house burned, and more would die and more houses would be burned unless the children's father was caught or killed.

The coffins were unloaded and placed on

ropes at the heads of the graves. Whatley opened his Bible. He began reading from it. Hickory listened with only a part of his mind. With the rest he kept wondering what he was going to do. As usual he found no answers.

Whatley finished reading and closed the Bible. He said, 'Vengeance is mine, saith the Lord. But the good book also says, "An eye for an eye, a tooth for a tooth." Well, the father of those two dead children there has had his eye for an eye, his tooth for a tooth. He has killed two men. He has burned the Jerrold house in vengeance for the burning of his village. Pray God that he will go away and leave us be.'

Half a dozen voices said softly, 'Amen.' Whatley nodded to the men manning the ropes and they lowered the coffins into the graves.

Whatley picked up a handful of earth and sifted part of it into each of the graves. Mrs Jerrold and Mrs Cheever wept softly as he did. Then he turned and headed down the slope toward town. The townspeople followed him. Kaminski and Cruthers began filling in the graves.

There were tears in Lila Anthony's eyes. She took Hickory's arm and walked beside him down the hill. Jess took his hand and walked on the other side. None of them spoke. There didn't seem to be anything to say.

CHAPTER EIGHT

The spring wagon passed Hickory and Lila before they reached the rear of the boardinghouse. By the time they reached the street, it had disappeared inside the livery barn. The mourners straggled back, the men mostly going into the saloon, the women and children into the boardinghouse. Hickory wondered where the Indian was. Was he watching from some knoll or had he gone for the day? Curious enough to check, he left Lila and Jeff and crossed the street to the livery. He got his horse from the corral, saddled, and rode out. A quarter mile from town he began a big circle, looking for the Indian's trail.

He had gone nearly halfway around town before he found it, the trail of an unshod pony looking like it was about ten hours old.

He dismounted and studied it, memorizing the prints from habit. The Indian pony had been traveling at a walk, as if the Indian had all the time in the world. 'Not today,' Hickory thought. 'Maybe when nobody follows you, mister, you'll get careless, and then will be the time to follow you.' He turned his horse back toward town.

A wagon with two horses hitched to it stood in front of the Erdman cabin just beyond the boardinghouse. Another stood in front of

Amos Ford's tarpaper shack next door. The Erdmans and Ford and his wife were carrying belongings out and loading the wagons with them.

Hickory rode to Erdman's wagon and sat his horse looking down. 'Leaving?'

Erdman stopped. He had four kids. They continued to carry things out, handing them to their mother, who stood in the wagon bed, a thin, haggard woman who was thirty-five but who looked twenty years older than that. Erdman said, 'You're damned right we are. There ain't nothin' here so good that we got to stay. We're takin' what we got and gettin' out. Amos an' Elsie are goin' along with us.'

Hickory said, 'You're on your own if you do. I won't guarantee the Indian won't attack you anyway.'

Erdman looked at him sourly. 'What are you guaranteein' the ones that stay?'

Hickory said, 'You're making a mistake.'

Erdman shrugged. 'Maybe. Only *I* figger it'd be a mistake to stay.'

'Want some help?'

'Don't need no help.'

Hickory nodded and rode next door. Amos and Elsie Ford were busy carrying things to the wagon. Being only two, they had fewer things than the Erdmans did. Hickory said, 'Need some help?'

Amos Ford, short and bald and sweating heavily, glanced up. 'Got 'er done. Thanks all the same.'

Hickory said, 'You're sure this is what you want to do? Just because you're not in town don't mean the Indian won't attack.'

'We'll take our chances.'

Hickory shrugged. Both families were firmly determined to leave and he couldn't say anything that would change their minds. Maybe they figured that by nightfall they'd be far enough away so that the Indian wouldn't bother them, but they were wrong. Two wagons, crawling along the road, couldn't make more than half a dozen miles before it got dark.

He rode back to the livery stable, unsaddled his horse, and put him into the corral. Chris Dobbs was pacing nervously back and forth, occasionally kicking the dry manure. He stopped long enough to ask, 'You find his trail?'

Hickory nodded.

'How old?'

'Eight, maybe ten hours. He rode out a long time before it got light.'

'You follow it?'

Hickory shook his head. 'Maybe if we don't follow it, he'll figure we're not going to. Maybe in a day or two he won't bother to ride twenty miles.'

'If there's anybody alive in Yellowhorse by then.'

Hickory said, 'Or anybody left. Erdman and

his family are leaving. So's Amos Ford.'

'That's eight. We buried two. Leaves twenty-six for the Indian.'

It wasn't funny, but Hickory grinned at him. Dobbs growled, 'Maybe I ought to keep busy making coffins. Looks like we might need some more.'

Hickory said, 'Don't. People are nervous enough as it is.'

He went out, leaving Dobbs still pacing back and forth. The townspeople had gathered around the two wagons and were saying good-bye to the Erdmans and the Fords. Mrs Ford, plump and good-humored, was weeping as she hugged first one and then another of her friends. Mrs Erdman's face was grim.

The four kids crawled up on the load and Erdman drove away, heading north. When this road hit the Arkansas it would connect with a better road heading west. Ford climbed to the seat, reached down a hand to his wife, then slapped the horses' backs with the reins. Both wagons creaked slowly out of town.

The remaining townspeople stood in the street, watching them. Somebody said, 'Maybe they're smart. Maybe that's what we all ought to do.'

Hickory started to say something, then closed his mouth. Trying to talk them out of leaving might only make them want to leave all the more. And besides, he wasn't sure but what they *would* be better off if they all left. At least some of them would remain alive, and once they lost themselves in a big town like Pueblo or Denver, they'd be safe.

The Indian would burn the town as soon as they had left, of course, and they'd lose everything they owned. But that could happen even if they stayed.

The wagons disappeared below a rise and the townspeople reluctantly dispersed. Some went to their homes for valuables they wanted to bring to the boardinghouse. Some of the men went back into the saloon. A few had already had too much to drink, but Hickory didn't say anything. The children congregated on the porch of the boardinghouse, subdued and scared. They didn't even seem to want to play.

Lila Anthony asked, 'Do you think they'll be all right?'

Hickory nodded. 'Probably. The Indian is likely twenty miles away.' But he knew the safety of the two families depended on which way the Indian returned to town. If he came back from the north, he'd probably see their dust and investigate. And, having a gun now, he could pick them off at will.

With the departure of the four Erdman children, nearly half of the town's children were gone. Remaining were Jess Anthony, the two Jerrold boys, the two yellow-haired Cruthers children, Hieda and Lars and Jennie and Frank Spence. Jess, being the youngest,

72

was largely ignored by the older kids.

Since it was close to noon, a good many of the families in Yellowhorse went home and began cooking dinner to save the quarter Mrs Cheever charged for every meal, but Hickory, Lila Anthony, and Jess went into the boardinghouse dining room and sat down. Lila said, 'The stage is due tomorrow. A lot more people are going to leave on it.'

Hickory nodded. 'I suppose.'

'And that will leave fewer here.'

He looked straight into her eyes. 'Why don't you take Jess and leave? You could stay in Denver until this is over with.'

Before she could reply, Mrs Cheever brought in a big bowl of stew and another of corn-on-the-cob she had raised in her vegetable garden behind the boardinghouse. Lila helped Jess and then herself and then handed the bowls to Hickory.

His left arm still ached from the blow of the Indian's rifle the night before. His hand hurt when he used it and it had stiffened some, but his ribs and chest hurt only when he twisted a certain way. None of it affected his appetite. He filled his plate and began to eat.

When he had finished, he pushed back his chair and got to his feet. 'I'm going around and warn everybody to put out their fires and bring all their matches here. There's no use making things easy for that damn Indian. You think about what I said.'

73

'There are some matches over at my place.'
'Tell me where they are and I'll bring them when I come back.'

She told him and he left. He started at the north end of town and stopped at every cabin, warning the occupants not to leave fires or matches for the Indian. He went to Lila's house and got her matches from the cupboard near the stove. He stopped at the stone-block jail and put Lila's matches in the drawer of his desk. It wouldn't do the Indian any good to try and burn down the jail and he probably wouldn't even try. Besides, once the jail was locked up it would be as difficult to break into as it was to break out of.

In front of Hickory's rolltop desk there was a swivel chair that could tilt back. He sat down, put his booted feet up on the desk, and lighted a cigar.

He closed his eyes. He stayed this way for a long time, then suddenly sat up straight. He got paper and pen out of his desk and wrote a letter to the commandant at Fort Lyon on the Arkansas. He asked for a troop of cavalry to be sent at once, describing briefly what had happened and why he thought it was happening. The cavalry wouldn't arrive for a week or more and the trouble would probably be all over by the time they did, but it was one active thing he *could* do. He put the letter into an envelope, addressed it, and put it into the pocket of his shirt. He'd give it to the stage driver tomorrow.

He wondered how many of the townspeople would be leaving on the stage. It would probably depend on how many were already traveling on it, but he was willing to bet that all seats would be filled when the stage pulled out.

He finished his cigar. The air in his office was blue with it. He got up and threw it into the stove, then sat down again and put up his feet. He pulled his hat down over his face and closed his eyes.

He dozed in snatches, always awaking with a start, sweating and cold. The Indian paraded through every dream, painted and half naked and as ferocious and cunning as any animal.

Hickory suddenly thought about the possibility of setting traps for the Indian and wondered if there were any bear traps in Jerrold's store. He got up, locked the jail door with the heavy padlock from the outside, and walked up the street toward Jerrold's store.

Setting a trap for a man was barbaric and doing it went against Hickory's nature, but he was desperate. The Cheyenne had to be caught or killed. One way or another he had to be stopped before he killed again.

Mrs Jerrold led him back to the storeroom at the rear of the store. There, hanging on a nail were three heavy bear traps big enough and strong enough to snap the leg bone on a man.

She knew what he wanted them for and refused to take money for them. She told him to take them and wished him success.

The three traps were heavy. Hickory slung the chains over his shoulder and went out. He stuck his head into the saloon. 'I need a couple of men.'

Several started toward him. He nodded at Harry Spence and at Juan Garcia because they seemed more sober than the others, and they came outside. He said, 'Harry, get a twelve-pound sledge from the blacksmith shop. Juan, get a pitchfork from the stable.'

They hurried away to obey. Hickory stared around the town, trying to select the most likely places to set the traps. In passageways, he thought, where the Indian will be forced to walk along a fairly narrow path. He crossed the street. There was a passageway between the livery stable and the shack next to it that wasn't much more than four feet wide.

Spence arrived with the sledge, Juan with the fork. Hickory drove the stake, then, with Garcia's help, set the trap. Having done so, he covered the cruel, rusty teeth with dead grass and weeds. He told Spence to stay with the trap until all the townspeople had been told where it was.

He and Garcia set the other two in two other passageways and he covered them similarly. Then, leaving Garcia to watch the second two, he went back to the saloon. He told everyone the locations of the traps and told them to spread the word. He told the children on the boardinghouse porch and he told the people who were inside.

Near sundown, everyone began assembling at the boardinghouse. When they had all arrived, he told everyone again about the traps and where each one was. Then he went out and yelled for Garcia and Spence to come in.

The two men did. Almost everybody had eaten at home before coming to the boardinghouse. Those who hadn't, went into the dining room for supper. Hickory was too nervous to eat. Holding his rifle, he sat in the deepening shadows of the boardinghouse veranda, staring at the darkening plain and wondering when the Indian would arrive.

The sky grew wholly dark. The boardinghouse blinds were drawn, the lamps inside turned as low as possible. Next door, the saloon doors were closed and the shades on the windows pulled.

Hickory wondered if he would hear the jaws of the trap that caught the Indian. He wondered if the man would yell.

Perhaps not, he thought, but he'd hear some kind of commotion. Tense, sometimes almost holding his breath, he waited for a sound that would tell him one of the traps had caught the Indian.

CHAPTER NINE

But it wasn't the sound of a trap being sprung that brought Hickory to his feet about ten o'clock. It was the sound of wagon wheels and horses' hoofs coming fast out of the north. He knew who it was even before the first team came into view. The Erdmans and the Fords were coming back, which could only mean one thing. They had been attacked.

He opened the door of the boardinghouse and said, 'Wagons coming.' He reached the saloon just as Amos Ford's shout rang out, 'Help, somebody! Erdman's shot and so's my wife!'

The two wagons pulled to a halt in front of the boardinghouse. Mrs Erdman harshly ordered her four children to go inside. Hickory leaned over the side of the wagon and felt for a pulse in Jim Erdman's throat. There was none. He looked up at Mrs Erdman. 'I'm sorry. He's dead.'

She showed no sign of grief. She stared at him in stony silence as if he was responsible. He said, 'Ma'am, go on into the boardinghouse. Your youngsters need you and I reckon you need them.'

He knew there would be those who would think she didn't care that Jim Erdman was dead, but he knew it wasn't true. She was

78

grieving in her own way, the grief bottled up where it couldn't show. She climbed down from the wagon, refusing Hickory's help. Ignoring him, she turned. Her hand went out briefly, gently, touched her husband's face. She withdrew it quickly, as if ashamed of having let her feelings show. She turned and stalked into the boardinghouse, bony and awkward and thin.

Mrs Ford was also shot. There was a gaping wound in her fleshy upper arm. Blood had run down her arm and onto her hand. It was smeared on her dress where she had wiped her hand. Her face was ghastly pale and her eyes betrayed her pain. Two men helped her down from the wagon seat and the women took over and helped her into the boardinghouse.

Hickory spoke to the men standing nearest him. 'Two or three of you carry him over across the street. Dobbs, you can start building a coffin now.'

A couple of men picked up Jim Erdman's body, which was very light for all his nearly six feet of height, and carried it into the boardinghouse. Hickory looked at Amos Ford. 'What happened?'

'Well, it was just about dark. Dusk, I guess. We was driving along and Jim was ahead and all of a sudden that damn redskin opened up on us from a gully. Knocked Jim down off the seat with his first shot. Threw two or three more at us and nicked Elsie with the last. She let out a screech and I shot a couple of times at where the Injun's gun flashes had been.'

'What then?'

'That was all. There wasn't no more shooting. I was pretty scared but I ran over to where the shots had come from to see if I'd hit the sonofabitch. He was waiting for me. His gun must of been empty. He swung it like a club. I ducked and he missed and I high-tailed it out of there. I didn't go back until I heard his horse leaving. When I did, my gun was gone and his was there.'

'How many cartridges left in your gun?'

'Well, you remember it. It was a Henry and I shot twice, but hell, I don't know whether the damn thing was full or not.'

'Then he could have as many as thirteen cartridges left in it.'

Ford looked sheepish. 'I wasn't thinking about my gun. I was looking to see if I'd hit him and all of a sudden he raised up in front of me, yellin' like something straight out of hell. I was so damn scared, I just dropped my gun and ran.'

Hickory nodded. 'All right. Go on in and stay with your wife.'

Ford went into the boardinghouse. Hickory unhitched first one team and then the other, leaving the wagons standing in front of the boardinghouse. They'd provide some protection from the Indian's bullets if he began shooting from across the street. Hickory tied the lathered heaving horses to the rail in front of the saloon, knowing they ought to be cooled before they were given a drink.

He went back and positioned himself behind the Ford wagon, his rifle resting on the sideboards in front of him. The Indian had killed three of the inhabitants of Yellowhorse and had wounded two. He'd burned a house and he apparently had no intention of giving up. Hickory caught himself whispering, 'Oh Lord, let him walk into one of the traps.'

He didn't suppose he ought to bring the Lord into it, but on the other hand there wasn't anything wrong with praying for people's lives and if the Indian wasn't caught more people were going to die.

Dobbs began sawing lumber across the street. Otherwise the town was quiet as a tomb. The horses' breathing had quieted. They stood with their heads hanging, not even bothering to switch their tails.

Suddenly Hickory heard a yell. It came from between the livery stable and the cabin next to it, where he had set the first bear trap. Immediately following the yell there was a high, shrill nicker of terror and pain from a horse, followed by a racket that sounded like a herd of wild horses crashing into the side of the livery barn.

Hickory cursed beneath his breath as he raised his rifle to eye level in case the Indian came bursting out into the street. The damn trap had caught the Indian's horse instead of the Indian himself. Now he'd be on guard. Now there was little chance of trapping him. He'd find the other traps and spring them. Worse, he'd be enraged at the loss of his horse. He'd need another ... Hickory was moving even as he had the thought. He circled the wagon and ran straight across the street. Men who had heard the commotion came running out of the saloon. One or two staggered after him, but Hickory yelled at them to go back.

He didn't wait to see if he had been obeyed. He ran through the weeds at the side of the livery stable, heading toward the corral at its rear. He was just in time to glimpse the Indian thundering out of the corral gate astride a bare-backed horse. He raised his rifle to his shoulder and snapped a shot at the fleeing Indian. He wasn't able to see his sights and had to content himself with simply pointing the gun. The Cheyenne didn't fall but Hickory knew he'd hit the man because of the way the Indian's body jerked.

He stopped and stared into the darkness. Frustration was strong in him. For the first time he'd had a good shot at the Indian and he'd only hit him in a non-vital spot. He'd have a hell of a time explaining that to the people huddled in the boardinghouse and the saloon.

The Indian's horse was still fighting the bear trap on the other side of the livery barn. Hickory closed the corral gate and then circled the corral, coming into the passageway from the rear.

It was a wonder the horse's leg hadn't separated. The terrified and pain-stricken animal was bucking and lunging against the chain, sometimes banging into the livery stable wall, each time with a thunderous crash.

Hickory approached cautiously. When he was close enough to be fairly sure of his aim, he raised his rifle, pointed it at the horse's neck, and fired. The horse collapsed forward and lay down on his side. His side heaved twice and after that was still.

Hickory went back and checked the corral gate to be sure he had barred it securely. Then he returned to the street. Men stood in front of the saloon and a few people were gathered on the porch of the boardinghouse. Hickory said loud enough for all to hear, 'His horse stepped in the bear trap. He stole another out of the corral.'

'What was all the shooting?' someone asked.

Hickory said, 'I shot at the Indian but I didn't bring him down. I used the other shot on his horse.'

He realized he was staring at them as if daring someone to make a remark. He grinned faintly to himself. He was edgy and on the prod. Someone grumbled, 'Christ, he had a shot at the sonofabitch and missed!'

Hickory opened his mouth to defend himself, then closed it without saying anything.

83

He hadn't brought the Cheyenne down and for practical purposes that was as bad as missing him. He said, 'All right, go back inside. Just because he stole a horse and rode away doesn't mean he's gone for the night.'

'What about the other traps?'

'We'll pick them up tomorrow. He'll be on the lookout for them now.'

Some of the men left the saloon and came to the boardinghouse. Others went back inside. Those who had gathered on the porch of the boardinghouse went back in. Hickory followed them. Tonight he asked Harry Spence to keep watch in an upstairs front bedroom and asked Frank Feeley to guard the rear. He himself settled down on a sofa facing the front door.

It was twenty minutes or so before everybody had disappeared upstairs. Lila Anthony and Jess had stayed behind. She sat down on the sofa beside Hickory and said, 'It's like he wasn't human. Or like God was on his side.' There was a kind of fearful awe in her voice.

Hickory said, 'He's human all right. So far he's just been lucky. But we'll get him.'

She nodded and rose. 'Good night.'

'Good night.' He stared at her and caught himself wondering what it would be like to go upstairs with her. He forced his thoughts back to the Indian and Lila walked on up the stairs with Jess.

Hickory wanted to think about Lila but he knew he had to keep his thoughts on the Indian. He had to try and guess what the savage would do next. If he could guess right, he'd have a chance of preventing the man from doing whatever he had planned.

He'd burn something, Hickory supposed, and that something would probably be Chris Dobbs's house. Or the boardinghouse. Or the livery barn, where Dobbs was working, guarded by two other men.

He shook his head reluctantly. There was no way he could anticipate the Indian's next action with any accuracy. And he didn't intend to go out and prowl the town alone. Last time he'd tried he'd nearly gotten killed for his pains.

He got up and turned the lamp low. He checked his rifle to be sure it was fully loaded. He sat down again, put his head back and closed his eyes. He kept telling himself that there had to be a way but he didn't know what it was.

He remembered the four horses that had been hitched to the wagons, still tied to the rail in front of the saloon. He ought to put them in the livery stable corral. Maybe when Dobbs and the two with him came back . . .

He dozed, awakening when the door of the boardinghouse opened and Dobbs came in. Dobbs said, 'What you going to do about those horses? Leave 'em there?'

Hickory got up. 'I'll put them in the corral. Come on and give me a hand.'

He headed toward the door, but before he could reach it, he heard a shrill neigh of terror from the corral behind the livery barn. He knew instantly what it was. The Indian, having been deprived of his own horse, was now systematically depriving the whites of Yellowhorse of theirs.

He burst from the boardinghouse door, thundered across the porch, and ran across the street. Turning his head, he yelled at Dobbs and at the two men who had been with Dobbs, 'Come on! He's in the corral and maybe we can get him this time!'

He plunged through the weeds and dry grass in the lot beside the livery barn, wishing there was more light. He drew his revolver and thumbed the hammer back.

Behind him, Dobbs and the others lagged, afraid, but Hickory didn't slow. He reached the corner of the livery barn and skidded to a halt.

The Cheyenne had worked swiftly and he had worked well. Four of the six horses that had been in the corral were down. One was bucking frantically around and around. The Indian was in the act of plunging his knife into the neck of the sixth. The animal was racing furiously around the corral while the Indian clung like a leech to his back, laying forward over his withers with an arm encircling

86

his neck.

Hickory climbed the corral fence, scrambling and clawing in his haste. He reached the top, steadied himself, and snap-fired his revolver as he did. The bullet struck the horse instead of the Indian and he plunged forward, throwing the Indian clear. Hickory found himself praying, 'God, let him be stunned. Let him stay down for just a second!'

The Indian hit the ground and rolled. In his eagerness, Hickory jumped down from the top rail of the corral.

He hit the ground running toward the Indian. Again he snapped a shot at the man, this time from a distance of no more than thirty feet.

He was rewarded by seeing the Indian falter as he struggled to his feet. Then the Indian leaped for the corral fence like a cat and scrambled to the top. Hickory fired again as his body was silhouetted against the sky. Then the man was gone, and all that remained of him was the sound of his running feet, brief, then fading and dying away.

Hickory slammed his gun back into its holster furiously. He cursed savagely and aloud. Spread-legged, he stared at the destruction in the corral.

All six horses were down, dying or soon to die. The only horses left in town were the four wagon horses he had forgotten to put away.

CHAPTER TEN

Hickory had never been more furious in his life, but only part of his anger was directed at the Indian. The rest was directed at himself. He'd had two chances at the savage tonight, and while he thought he'd hit the Cheyenne twice, neither bullet seemed to have even slowed him down.

Chris Dobbs and the others came running now that the Indian had gone. Dobbs yelled, 'What the hell's the matter with you? You shot at him three times!'

Hickory whirled furiously. 'God damn it, don't you jump on me! Where the hell were you?'

'Comin'. By God, we was comin' just as fast as we could.'

'Sure. As fast as you could,' Hickory said disgustedly.

The three men stared at the destruction in the corral. Dobbs said, 'What we need is a new sheriff. One that can shoot.'

Hickory clenched his fists. After a moment he said as quietly as he could, 'Get one then. I resign.' He shoved the revolver back into the holster and unpinned the sheriff's badge from his shirt. He threw it into the corral manure at Chris Dobbs's feet. He said, 'I didn't have nothing to do with the deaths of those Indian kids. But you did and so did everybody else who went into that carnival tent and didn't protest what was being done to them.' He turned and stalked angrily to the corral gate.

He went through it and ten yards beyond before Chris Dobbs called, 'Wait a minute! No call to get so damn proddy.'

Hickory didn't stop and he didn't look back.

He heard feet running behind him. The three men caught up. Dobbs said, 'Wait a minute! I flew off the handle is all.' He was wiping manure off the sheriff's badge on his pants. He said, 'I'm sorry. Hell, everybody knows you're doin' the best you can.'

The two with Dobbs added their voices to his. 'He didn't mean nothing, Hickory. Take the badge and put it back on. Nobody could've done no better than you.'

Hickory took the badge but he didn't pin it on. He dropped it into the pocket of his shirt.

The shots and commotion had aroused everybody. They were clustered in front of the saloon and on the veranda of the boardinghouse. Questions were thrown at Hickory and he didn't wait for the criticism he knew was sure to come. He said defiantly, his anger plain in his voice. 'All right! I shot at him three times and all I did was nick him again.' He took the badge out of his pocket. 'You'd all better make up your minds right now whether you want me to stay on as sheriff or not. If you do want me to stay on, I don't want to hear you bellyaching every time anything goes wrong. If my best ain't good enough, then by God you get somebody else!'

There was complete silence from the townspeople. Hickory strode to the saloon and banged inside. Marsh Haggerty followed, leaving the townspeople silent in the street. Hickory said disgustedly, 'Give me a drink!'

Haggerty slid him a bottle and glass. Hickory dumped the glass half full. He gulped it, anger still seething in him. He poured and drank a second, wiped his mouth, and then unexpectedly grinned at Haggerty. He said, 'The hell of it is, I'm madder at myself than I am at them. I *should* have got that sonofabitch even if there wasn't any light. He wasn't no farther from me than from here to the end of the bar.'

Haggerty said, 'You was probably trying too damn hard.'

Hickory nodded. Chris Dobbs came into the saloon, followed by William Whatley. Dobbs said, 'They voted. They want you to stay on.'

Whatley said, 'Nobody could have done more than you have, Hickory. Nobody else would have gone out after him alone.'

Hickory scowled, but he nodded. 'All right.'

Dobbs's voice showed his extreme relief. He asked, 'What about them four horses, Hickory? They're the only horses left in town.'

'Water them and get them some hay. But leave 'em tied in front of the saloon.'

90

Dobbs hurried away to obey.

Whatley said, 'I'm going to pray for help from the Lord.'

'What kind of help? You going to ask him to kill the Indian? I got a sneaking hunch the Lord might be on his side.'

Whatley said disapprovingly, 'That's blasphemy! The Lord on the side of a cold-blooded murderer?'

'Maybe the Lord is taking his vengeance through that Indian. You ever think of that?' He didn't believe it but he didn't like Whatley's pious attitude.

Whatley said, 'You are reproaching me for the deaths of those two Indian children, aren't you?'

Hickory nodded. 'Maybe I am. Maybe I am at that.'

'What would you have done if you had been here?'

'I'd have got 'em out of that cage the minute I knew they were there. I'd have had 'em in bed twenty-four hours sooner and it just might've made a difference.' He poured himself another drink. His hands were steadier. His anger had cooled and he realized that putting blame on Whatley or on anybody else wouldn't help anyone. He gulped the drink, paid Haggerty, and went out. He went next door to the boardinghouse and stepped inside.

Nearly everybody had gone back to bed. Lila was waiting for him near the door. He asked, 'Where's Jess?'

'Upstairs in bed. I stayed to talk to you.'

He grinned at her. 'I'm all right now. I was mad, but I got over it.'

'They don't mean to criticize. It's just that they're afraid.'

His grin widened. 'I don't blame 'em. I am myself.'

'Do you think he'll be back tonight?'

'He'll be back. He's lost his horse and he's hurt. He's likely madder than a teased rattlesnake.'

'What do you think he'll do this time?'

'Burn something if he's got anything to start a fire with.' He was wondering where he had hit the Indian. Maybe the man was hurt badly enough to even up the odds.

She stood on tiptoe and kissed him on the mouth. 'Be careful, Hickory. Don't let what Dobbs and the others said make you do something reckless.'

'All right.' He watched her go up the stairs approvingly, liking the way she moved. When this was over with, he thought, he'd damn sure find out if he was too old for her or not. He'd ask her, and he had a notion her answer would be what he wanted it to be. But then hell, a man never knew what was in a woman's mind. Times when he thought he knew was when he turned out to be most wrong.

He sat down and closed his eyes, with the uneasy feeling that this would be a long night with little sleep for him. And he wasn't long finding out that he'd been right. Lila Anthony came running down the stairs, her face white, her eyes wide with terror. 'Hickory! He's gone!'

'Who's gone? What are you talking about?'

'Jess! I left him upstairs and he's gone!'

Hickory was on his feet. He took the stairs two at a time. He burst into Lila's room, going to the window immediately. It was closed, and locked. He said, 'He wasn't taken, if that's what you were thinking. He's probably right here in the boardinghouse.'

'But where? And why would he leave the room?'

It was too soon for anybody to have gone back to sleep. Lila called down the hallway for Jess and Hickory added his voice to hers. They received no reply. Hickory hurried downstairs, with Lila following. One by one, starting with the kitchen, they searched the downstairs rooms. Hickory asked, 'Could he be teasing? Does he ever hide from you?'

She shook her head, the terror back in her eyes.

Hickory was beginning to get scared himself. It was obvious that Jess wasn't in the boardinghouse. The Cheyenne hadn't taken him, which could only mean one thing. Jess had left the boardinghouse voluntarily during the commotion a few minutes before. Why he'd left was anybody's guess.

Facing the certainty that Jess had left of his

own accord, Hickory asked himself where the boy could have gone. The answer to that was obvious. He would have gone home. There must have been something there that he wanted, and he had gone to get it.

He said, 'Stay here,' and crossed the parlor at a run. He snatched up his rifle and burst from the door. The four horses were tied to one of the wagons, between it and the boardinghouse. The contents of the wagon had been put into the other and the wagon bed filled with hay which the horses were eating hungrily. Hickory crossed the street at a run, heading for Lila's house.

What better revenge for the Indian, he thought, than to kill one of the townspeople's children in retaliation for the deaths of his own?

He heard running footsteps behind him and stopped, whirling toward the sound. It was Lila, running, holding up her skirts to keep from tripping on them. He caught her as she reached him. Her cheeks were wet with tears and he had never seen more terror in another human's eyes. He said, 'Go back. I'll look for him.'

'No!' Her voice was very near a scream. 'I'll help! I've got to help!'

He gripped her arms and shook her angrily. 'I said go back! I can't do Jess any good if I have to watch out for you!'

'I'm all right. You don't have to watch out

for me! Just let me go! Let me look for him!'

'Damn it, do what I say!' His voice was almost a shout. It stopped her tears. It made her look at him, seeing him for the first time. He said, 'I'll find him, but I can't if I have to worry about you. Now go back. We're losing time.'

She slumped and nodded numbly. He released her and she turned and went back across the street. He didn't wait to see if she went inside, but turned and ran through the grass and weeds toward her house beyond.

He almost collided with Jess, running toward him from the house. He grabbed the boy, who was carrying a red-and-black cast-iron toy locomotive. He stared into the darkness in the direction of Lila's house. He said harshly, 'Do you know you nearly scared your ma to death?'

He didn't see any movement and he heard no sound. But he knew better than to turn his back. Holding Jess, he backed toward the street.

Lila must have seen Jess. He heard her call and released the boy who immediately ran across the street and into his mother's arms.

The Indian did not appear so he turned and hurried to where Lila was, kneeling on the ground, arms around Jess, weeping almost hysterically with relief. Hickory knelt beside her. 'I thought you were told to stay with your ma.'

Jess's voice was scared. 'I wanted my train.'

'Did you see anybody?'

'I saw an Indian. All painted up.'

'Did he hurt you?'

Jess's chin began to quiver and tears welled up into his eyes. 'He scared me.'

'Did he touch you?'

'He picked me up.'

'But he put you down?'

Jess nodded wordlessly.

Hickory said, 'Take him in to bed. Good night.'

Lila picked Jess up and carried him inside. Hickory stared into the darkness. The Indian could have killed Jess but he had not.

Suddenly Hickory wished he and the Cheyenne didn't have to be mortal enemies. But there wasn't any help for it. He had to kill the Indian if he could and the Indian would try his best to kill him. It could be no other way.

CHAPTER ELEVEN

For a long while, Hickory slouched on the sofa, eyes closed, mind alert and wide awake. The Indian was still here. Jess had seen him. And if he was here, he would attempt further destruction.

The horses in the corral were dead and he would not again try to enter the boardinghouse by an upstairs window, knowing men were on guard. Fire, then, had to be what he'd try.

Hickory kept opening his eyes, staring toward the front windows. But he saw no glow and finally he went to sleep.

Occasionally during the night he awakened, usually because of pain either in his hand, his bruised arm, or in the bound-up knife slashes across his ribs and chest. Once he got up and went to the window, pulled aside the blind and looked outside. It seemed like any other quiet, peaceful night, except for the two wagons parked in front of the boardinghouse and except for the four horses tied to the wagon wheels munching hay out of the wagon bed.

Either the Indian had grown tired of terrorizing the town for tonight or else he'd had no matches with which to start a fire. In either case, he seemed to be gone. Hickory went back to the sofa, stretched out and made himself comfortable. He promptly went to sleep.

When he awakened, the room was light. The blinds had been raised and the boardinghouse parlor was full of people. Lila and Jess sat in a chair facing him. Lila smiled at him as he opened his eyes. She said, 'I'm glad you slept. You needed it.'

Hickory looked at the wall clock and saw that it was almost eight o'clock. He sat up, stretched and rubbed his eyes. Lila said, 'Want some coffee?'

He nodded. She left to get him a cup. Jess studied him with sober eyes. Hickory said, 'The Indian picked you up, you say. Did he hurt you?'

Jess shook his head. Hickory asked, 'How long did he hold you? Very long?'

Again Jess shook his head.

Hickory grinned. 'Did you yell?'

'Uh uh. I was too scared.'

Hickory thought it was probably a good thing Jess hadn't yelled. Lila brought the coffee and he sipped it gratefully.

He suddenly heard the sound of a saw across the street. Dobbs was working on Jim Erdman's coffin, he supposed. Mrs Erdman sat in a back corner of the boardinghouse parlor. Her face was stony. Her four children sat, cowed, on the sofa at her side.

Hickory looked at Lila Anthony. 'How's Mrs Ford this morning?'

'All right. Her arm pains her, but she doesn't complain.'

Hickory finished the coffee and got to his feet. He went out into the sunlight. The horses had pretty well cleaned up the hay that had been put into the wagon bed for them. There was a fresh, early-morning smell in the air. Today, he thought, was the day the weekly stage came in, and by tonight there would be fewer people left in Yellowhorse.

He walked slowly toward the jail, thinking how unreal it was that a single man could

98

terrorize an entire town. There ought to be some way he could be stopped, but Hickory couldn't think what it would be. He thought of the letter to the commandant at Fort Lyon. He could at least get it on the stage today and it should reach Fort Lyon by tomorrow.

He reached the jail, unlocked it, and went inside. He washed in cold water, shaved, and put on a clean shirt. He sat down in his swivel chair and lighted a cigar.

Why hadn't the Indian burned something last night, he asked himself. The savage must have some way of making fire even if he carried no matches with him. He had flint, and steel, and he could kindle a fire whenever he wanted to.

It must be, he decided, that the Indian was enjoying himself. He was playing a game with the people of Yellowhorse. He was letting them sweat it out, making themselves jumpy and nervous worrying about what he would do next.

And he was succeeding admirably. Hickory knew the Indian could burn the entire town if he wanted to. All he had to do was wait for a windy night and then fire a building on the upwind side of town. Wind and sparks would take care of the rest and the people wouldn't come out to fight the flames because they'd be afraid. When fire finally drove them out, the Indian would be waiting for them.

Angrily Hickory threw the half-smoked

cigar into the spittoon. He got up and went out, locking the door behind him.

Even before he reached the boardinghouse, he could hear William Whatley's voice. Whatley was holding church services even though it was only Thursday. Hickory didn't go in, partly because he didn't want to interrupt, partly because he figured that if he did, Whatley would start preaching straight at him.

Whatley said, 'Let us pray.' There was a short pause and a rustle as people shifted position, some kneeling, some only bowing their heads. Across the street the sound of Chris Dobbs building Jim Erdman's coffin went on.

Whatley said, 'Oh Lord, take mercy on us and deliver us from this scourge you have visited on us. We sinned against those children, Lord, and we know we did wrong. But it ain't been so long, Lord, since black people was slaves down south, and folks are mostly used to mindin' their own business. I know that ain't much excuse, but there's already been a lot of killin' of innocent folks. Dan Jerrold was a good man and left a family, and Len Cheever and Jim Erdman was good men too.'

He went on, but Hickory wasn't listening. He crossed the street and went into the livery stable. Chris Dobbs looked up from his work. One coffin was already finished and he was starting on another one. Hickory asked,

'Who's that for?'

'How do I know who it's for? I reckon only the redskin knows that and I ain't sure he does. Maybe only the Lord knows who's goin' to lie in this coffin I'm building now.'

Hickory said, 'I want you to quit it. It upsets folks to hear you building coffins. It's like somebody was building a scaffold out in the street.'

'Maybe that's what we ought to build. So the Injun will know what plans we got for him.'

Hickory said, 'Quit it. Time enough to build another coffin when somebody needs the goddam thing.'

Dobbs straightened. He said, 'You tend to your business and I'll tend to mine. Right now, my business is building coffins. Yours is catching that murdering Indian. If you'd do your job better, then maybe I wouldn't have to do mine.'

Hickory stared at the defiant Dobbs. He understood that Dobbs had to keep his hands busy to keep his mind off the Indian. But he also knew that if Dobbs went on as he was, he'd have half a dozen coffins built and that wasn't going to help the way the townspeople felt. Some of them were already close to the breaking point. If they had to listen to Dobbs sawing and hammering all day, knowing what he was doing, by nightfall they'd be half out of their minds.

But he couldn't force Dobbs to desist. He

101

started to leave, then paused and looked at Dobbs. 'There's better ways you can spend your time. If I was you, I'd hitch up one of those wagons and haul your valuables from your house over to the boardinghouse. He's burned Jerrold's house and he's killed all the horses in the corral. What do you figure he's going to do next?'

Dobbs put down his saw. No longer was there defiance in his eyes. He hurried out and Hickory followed. Dobbs went across the street. The wagon that had held hay for the horses was the one Amos Ford had driven yesterday. Dobbs went into the boardinghouse. He came out shortly and began unloading Ford's wagon onto the veranda of the boardinghouse.

Hickory leaned his rifle against the wall and helped. When the wagon was unloaded, Hickory said, 'Let's bring Erdman's coffin over and carry it into the boardinghouse.'

He helped Dobbs hitch a team to the wagon and rode across the street to the livery barn. They loaded the coffin, then took it back across the street. They carried it into the boardinghouse parlor and put it down. Whatley would take care of having Jim Erdman's body put into it after his wife had seen to it that he was dressed properly.

Dobbs's wife came out and Dobbs helped her up to the wagon seat. Hickory asked, 'Want some help?'

Dobbs nodded. 'I'd be obliged.'

Hickory sat on the endgate of the wagon as it jolted up the street and along the narrow, two-track road that led to Dobbs's house. Dobbs halted it in front. The three went inside and began carrying things out. Mrs Dobbs supervised, telling them which things she valued most. It was an odd assortment of things, Hickory thought, and the value Mrs Dobbs placed on things had no relationship to their actual value in dollars and cents.

They worked steadily for over an hour, until the wagon was piled high. Then, reluctantly, Mrs Dobbs agreed to stop. Dobbs helped her up on the wagon seat and drove back toward the boardinghouse. Hickory stayed behind. He remembered the traps and went to where they were set, springing each with a stick. The jaws snapped shut so viciously that he jumped each time. He knew there was no use leaving them. By now the Cheyenne probably knew exactly where they were, and they constituted a greater danger to the town's kids than they did to the Indian.

He looked at his watch. It was eleven o'clock and the stage was due at noon. He wished there were half a dozen stages coming through, and that every man, woman and child in Yellowhorse could be evacuated. But they couldn't. Most would have to stay, maybe all. It would depend on how many seats were available in the coach.

He returned to the boardinghouse. Several men and women were helping the Dobbses unload. Hickory found several men inside the saloon and said, 'Those horses have got to be dragged away or they'll be stinking up the town by tomorrow. I need a couple of men.'

Olaf Cruthers and Harry Spence volunteered. They followed Hickory out, and while Hickory unhitched the team from the wagon, they untied the other two and drove them across the street toward the livery barn.

Hickory drove his team over and got two logging chains out of the stable. He drove them back to the corral. Cruthers and Spence were waiting for the chains and immediately hooked onto the hind legs of one of the dead horses. Cruthers drove straight away from town and Hickory followed. Spence stayed behind.

Cruthers didn't stop until he was a quarter mile from town. Then he unhooked the chain from the dead horse and headed back.

It was almost noon by the time they had finished. They returned the horses to the rail in front of the boardinghouse, after watering them at the trough. Then Hickory lighted a cigar and stood there in the sun, waiting for the stage.

CHAPTER TWELVE

At five minutes before twelve, he saw a cloud of dust on the road south of town, and a couple of minutes after that, the dust materialized into four trotting horses and a rocking, weather-beaten coach.

By now, everyone in town had gathered to watch the stage arrive. Women and kids were in front of the boardinghouse, men mostly in front of the saloon. Usually the coach changed horses here, but today it would be impossible. The relief horses were dead, killed by the Indian. There were more horses out at Cruthers' ranch, but that was fifteen miles from town.

Just outside of town, the driver whipped his horses into a gallop, and that was the way he came in, yelling at the horses, cracking his whip, raising a mountainous cloud of dust.

He hauled the teams to a halt in front of the boardinghouse and the dust cloud rolled forward, obscuring coach and horses, covering the spectators and making them cough. But they wouldn't have had it any other way. The arrival of the stage was the high point of the week. The driver could have entered town with his horses at a trot but that wouldn't have been any fun for anyone.

Dobbs stepped out and held the bridle of the

lead horse and the driver climbed stiffly down. He was gray with dust. He nodded at Hickory. 'Howdy, Sheriff. Any passengers or freight?'

'Might be. How near are you to bein' full?'

'Got room for one, maybe two, if I crowd 'em in.' He went back and opened the coach door. 'Dinner stop, folks. Step right inside. Outhouses an' washstand are out in the back.'

The passengers began to disembark. They trotted into the boardinghouse, looking weary and beaten and covered with a fine film of dust. One man, in a dusty business suit and black derby hat, stopped before going in. He studied the loaded wagon standing in front of the boardinghouse and the four harnessed horses standing tied at the rail. He walked a few steps to the corner of the building and stared up the rise toward the cemetery where someone was working on Jim Erdman's grave. He returned to the sheriff. 'Someone die, sheriff?'

Hickory said drily, 'That's usually why you dig a grave.'

'How'd it happen? Looks like there's two more fresh graves up there. You got sickness in this town?'

Hickory said, 'You'll miss your dinner if you don't get on in the boardinghouse. They won't wait for you.'

'Yeah.' The man turned and started to go in, stopped when the driver called to Dobbs. 'Where's the fresh horses, Chris?'

Dobbs looked at Hickory. Hickory glanced

at the man in the derby hat, waiting for him to go on inside. But the man was intrigued and didn't move. The driver said, 'Where's the relief horses?'

Dobbs said, 'There ain't any. You'll have to get along without 'em.'

'What the hell happened to them? The next stage station is twenty miles.'

The stranger in the derby hat said, 'Something's going on here. What is it, sheriff?'

Hickory said, 'No concern of yours.' He turned and walked next door to the saloon. The driver followed him, frowning. The stranger began talking to Dobbs.

Hickory ordered a beer for himself and for the driver. The driver took a long gulp and looked inquiringly at Hickory, who said, 'We got a little Injun trouble. Killed all the horses in the corral last night.'

'How many?'

'Horses or Indians?'

'Indians. How many of 'em?'

'One.' Hickory took the letter to the commandant at Fort Lyons out of his pocket and handed it to the driver. 'See this gets to Fort Lyon as soon as possible. He's already killed three men.'

'Can't you catch the sonofabitch?'

'It's like trying to catch a shadow. I went out after him night before last and he damn near cut me to bits before I got away.'

'Can't you track him down?'

'Uh huh. He makes a trail out away from town but he doubles back. When dark comes, he's back in town.'

'What's he want? What's he doin' it for?'

'Long story. If you're going to eat, you'd better get over to the boardinghouse.'

'Sure.' The driver studied him a moment, then drained his beer mug and went out the door. Marsh Haggerty said, 'He'll find out. Somebody'll tell him.'

'Probably will.'

'And he'll talk about it all the way up the line. It might even get into the newspapers.'

'What if it does?'

'If it does that's the end of Yellowhorse.'

'So what if it is?'

Haggerty said, 'I'll tell you what. Every damn thing I got is tied up in this here town. I got a hundred and sixty acre homestead half a mile south, and half of another just behind the saloon. If everybody moves away, I'll be sittin' on two hundred and forty acres of nothin'.'

Hickory said, 'People forget.'

'Not something like this, they don't.'

Hickory said, 'I'll talk to him. I'll tell him to keep still.'

'You think he will?'

'Sure. Don't worry about it.' He got up and went out. The man in the derby hat stood across the street looking at the gaunt, blackened remains of the Jerrold house. He

108

saw Hickory and crossed the street to him. 'Looks like you had a fire.'

Hickory said, 'Looks like it.'

'Somebody get killed in the fire?'

'Nope.'

'There's a woman inside with a bloody bandage on her arm.'

Hickory nodded. 'Mrs Ford.'

'How'd it happen?'

Hickory stared at him. 'Who are you, anyway? Why all the questions?'

'I'm Ezra Logan. I work for the *Rocky Mountain News*.'

Hickory said, 'Mind your own business.'

'Mindin' my business ain't my job, and I smell a story here.'

Hickory said, 'Smell away.' He went into the boardinghouse. The townspeople were clustered in the parlor. The coach passengers were in the dining room. Hickory said, 'The driver says he's got room for two. No more. Who wants to go?'

A dozen people all spoke at once. Hickory said, 'You all can't go. All that want to, go over to the other side of the room.'

People crowded over to the other side of the room. Those who did not, looked uncertain, as if they'd also like to go. Hickory said, 'Families with more than two people can't go.'

The families with children reluctantly returned. Amos Ford and his wife, Max Kaminski and his wife, Frank and Mrs Feeley, and Herm Burge, who must be well over seventy and who lived alone in a one-room shack behind Jerrold's store, all remained. Hickory said, 'Work it out amongst yourselves. Might be you could ride up with the driver, Herm, if you think you're up to it.'

He went outside. Lila had made no move to join those who planned to leave. She hadn't even looked as if she wanted to.

The reporter, Logan, was lounging on the porch, smoking a cigar. He said, 'You'd just as well tell me the story, Sheriff. I'll get it before I'm through.'

'No you won't. The stage is leaving in twenty minutes.'

'But I'm not. I'm staying here. I smell a big one and I'm not leaving until I get it.'

Hickory sighed. 'All right. Last winter a carnival came through here. The guy who owned it was one of the volunteers in that Indian scrap up north.'

'Yeah. He was found with his throat cut about two months ago. Inside his carnival tent down on Ferry Street. And that wasn't all. Some parts of him was missing. Raised a hell of a stink at the time.'

Hickory nodded. 'He captured two little Indian kids in the fight. Put 'em in cages and exhibited them along with the animals he had. Brought 'em here. But they both were sick. Mrs Anthony got them out of their cages and put them to bed, but by then it was too late.

110

They died.'

'Where was you all this time? Why didn't you put a stop to it?'

'I was out of town.'

'What about the other people? Didn't anybody say anything?'

Hickory shook his head.

'And now the kids' pa is here looking for revenge. Is that it?'

'Looks like it.'

'And he's got three so far. Is he the one that killed all the horses but those four?'

Hickory nodded. He didn't like giving the story to Logan, but he knew he couldn't have kept the reporter from getting it if he'd tried.

The man breathed, 'Christ! What a story!'

'It won't do the town of Yellowhorse any good.'

Logan stared at him incredulously: 'You mean you want me to suppress it? Are you out of your mind?'

'What good will it do anybody?'

'Well, first of all, it'll get me a whopping raise and maybe job offers from half the eastern newspapers.'

Hickory said, 'This town is all these people have. Everything they've got is tied up here. You print a story like that and any chances Yellowhorse has got of growing will be gone. It'll wither. When the railroads come and the stagelines die the town will dry up and blow away.'

'Tough. They should've thought of that when those two little Indian kids were dying in their cage.'

Hickory shrugged. 'All right. But you'd better leave when the stage does.'

'Uh huh. Not until I get it all.'

'There isn't another stage for a week. There's no horses in town that you can buy or hire. You'll be stuck here with the rest of us.'

'A week's not so long.'

'The Indian won't know you from one of the townspeople.'

Logan didn't say anything but some of his self-assurance had evaporated. Hickory said, 'And don't expect friendliness from the people here.'

Logan said stubbornly, 'I'm staying and you're not going to talk me out of it. This is the opportunity of a lifetime.'

Hickory shrugged. He couldn't put the reporter on the stage by force. The driver came out of the boarding-house, followed by the passengers. It was apparent that none of them had noticed anything.

Amos Ford and his wife were the ones who were leaving on the stage. Hickory didn't know how it had been decided, but he supposed those who had wanted to leave had probably drawn straws. Herm Burge had received permission from the driver to ride up on the seat with him. He climbed up without too much difficulty and settled himself to wait while the driver put the

Fords' two carpetbags into the boot and laced the canvas over them.

He climbed to the seat, grinned down at Hickory, and cracked his long whip out over the heads of the lead team. They lunged into the harness and the coach started with a jerk.

At a gallop, he took them out of town, leaving a pall of dust lying over the length of the street, but just behind the last building he pulled them back to a trot. They had to go another twenty miles and he didn't intend to waste the strength that they had left.

Hickory looked around. He didn't see Ezra Logan and supposed he was either in the boardinghouse dining room or in the saloon.

He stuck his head into the boardinghouse. William Whatley was standing there talking to Jim Erdman's wife. Hickory said, 'Let's get on with the burying, Mr Whatley.'

'Yes. Yes of course,' he patted Mrs Erdman comfortingly on the shoulder. He directed four men to carry the casket out. Hickory watched the procession form, and wagon and mourners wound their way up the rise to the cemetery. Logan came out of the saloon and watched. Marsh Haggerty came out too and stood behind him, wiping his hands on his soiled apron and scowling at Logan's back.

Looking at Hickory he said in a voice loud enough for Logan to hear, 'You know what that dirty sonofabitch is goin' to do, Hickory? He's goin' to spread this whole story on the front page of the Denver newspaper.'

Logan didn't look around, but his neck turned red. Haggerty said threateningly, 'If he gets out of town in one piece, that is. Maybe the Injun will stick a knife in his goddam back.'

It sounded like it was only talk. But Hickory couldn't help remembering his two hundred and forty acres within half a mile of town.

CHAPTER THIRTEEN

Now that the stagecoach had left, most of the townspeople headed for the boardinghouse dining room to eat. Logan went into the saloon. Hickory, suspecting that trouble would follow Logan wherever he went, followed him.

Marsh Haggerty had gone back into the saloon. He stood behind the bar, glowering at Logan. Hickory stepped up beside the newspaperman. Haggerty ignored Logan's order for a drink, but when Hickory asked for a beer he drew it and slid it down the bar to him. Logan said, 'I'll have one too, bartender,' and Haggerty replied shortly. 'You can go straight to hell, mister. I ain't servin' the likes of you!'

Logan looked at Hickory, who said with a shrug, 'He's the bartender.'

Logan's face was getting red and his eyes

were narrow with anger. 'Isn't this a public place? And isn't a public place required to serve everyone?'

Haggerty said, 'We don't serve drunks.'

Logan started to open his mouth, then realized the futility of doing so.

Hickory asked, 'What good's it going to do to spread this story all over your newspaper? Why hurt *this* town? Dan Jerrold's widow owns this saloon and the store next door. Len Cheever's widow owns the boardinghouse. Spread a story like this and the first thing that will happen will be that the stagecoach quits stopping here. Even if we catch the Indian, people will be afraid to settle here. Everything these people have will be lost.'

Logan said, 'It's news and my job is to report the news.'

Hickory said, 'The people here don't show it, but they're damn desperate because they don't know what to do. Give 'em half a chance and they'll take their mad at the Indian out on you.'

'It's up to you to see that they don't do that.'

'I can't always be around. Matter of fact, I'm leaving town right away. I'm going out to Cruthers' ranch and bring some horses in. The Indian killed all of ours but those four wagon horses out in front.' He looked at Cruthers, standing near the end of the bar. 'How about it, Olaf? Couldn't we ride out to your place and bring some saddle horses in?'

'Sure, if you'll put a guard on 'em at night. I don't want their throats cut like the bunch in the corral last night.'

Hickory looked at Logan. 'You'd better come along. I can't look after you if I'm not in town.'

Logan's mouth was thin with anger, but he nodded. 'All right.'

Hickory finished his beer and wiped his mouth. He said, 'Come on,' and went out the door. It was near one o'clock but they'd have plenty of time if they only rode the wagon horses out and then came back on some of Cruthers' fresh saddle horses. Hickory was thinking about trying to run the Indian down tomorrow. It wasn't likely to work, but it would give the men something to do.

Each led one of the big wagon horses across the street to the livery barn, took the harness off, and saddled up. Cruthers rode out in the lead, forcing the wagon horse into a bone-jolting trot. The stirrups were too long for Logan's short legs but Hickory didn't offer to stop and adjust them for him. Let him get a sore rump and let him chafe the insides of his thighs. To hell with him.

What angered Hickory about Logan was his unfairness in laying all the blame on Yellowhorse. Yellowhorse wasn't the first town the carnival had visited. The thing had probably been in Denver for several weeks. It had probably visited Pueblo and all the little settlements in between. It had just been Yellowhorse's misfortune that the Indian children picked this place to die.

Riding behind Logan, he called, 'That carnival was based in Denver. How come you didn't pick up the story of the Indian kids while it was there?'

'I did.'

'And you printed it?'

'Sure I did.'

'And what happened?'

'The governor's office told the owner to get it out of town.'

'But nobody did anything about the Indian kids?'

'No. What could they do?'

Hickory said, 'We just got through fighting a war to free the slaves. They could have freed those kids.'

'They weren't slaves. They weren't being forced to work.'

Hickory said, 'That's splitting hairs.'

'Maybe so. But what would they have done with those two kids? Nobody in Denver wanted them. They were little savages and they'd likely have killed anyone who took them in.'

'You could've turned them loose.'

'They'd have died. They'd never have been able to reach their families.'

'They died anyway. And what makes their dying such big news all of a sudden?'

117

Logan said, 'It's not their dying that I consider news. It's their father taking vengeance against the town he blames for their death.'

Hickory said, 'You'd just better see to it that *you* stay in after dark. He ain't particular who he kills.'

They rode in silence after that. The afternoon wore away, and around four o'clock they saw Cruthers' horse ranch up ahead.

It consisted mostly of corrals, but there was a sod house that was occupied by Cruthers' two hired hands. There were thirty or forty horses in one of the corrals and a man was breaking one in an adjoining corral. The horse was bucking but before they reached the corral he stopped and stood, head down, trembling. His rider touched him in the ribs and raised his head by pulling on the reins and the horse began to walk docilely around the corral.

Cruthers called to the men, one of whom was standing beside the gate, 'Cut out eight or ten that are broke. We'll ride three and trail the others.'

Hickory swung down from the wagon horse. He took off his saddle and bridle and released the horse, knowing he would find his way back to town. He carried them to the corral gate and when one of Cruthers' men brought a horse out, he threw his saddle on and cinched it down. He put his bridle on, then took the rope off the horse's neck so that Cruthers' man

118

could coil it up.

Cruthers took the second horse out and Logan took the third. Cruthers' men began making up a string of the others, tying the halter rope of one to the tail of another, until they had half a dozen in a line.

The three rode out toward town, and again Hickory held to a steady trot, wanting to reach Yellowhorse well before dark. They arrived just as the sun was going down, dismounted in front of the boardinghouse, and tied the horses, one by one, to the rail in front of it and to the rail in front of the saloon. The Indian could, of course, kill the horses by shooting them, but Hickory didn't believe he would waste his cartridges on horses. He'd save them for the people of Yellowhorse.

Not having eaten dinner at noon, Hickory discovered he was hungry. He went into the boardinghouse and Logan followed him.

Lila Anthony was working in the dining room. Jess was playing in the corner of the room with his cast-iron train. Hickory sat down and Logan sat next to him. Lila stopped beside them. 'There's warmed-over beef stew from dinner. And dried apple pie.'

Hickory nodded. 'Sounds fine.'

She asked, 'What are the horses for?'

Hickory said, 'I thought maybe tomorrow we'd try and run the Indian down. It probably won't work, but it's worth trying.'

Lila left and went to the kitchen for their

food. Logan asked, 'What will you do with him if you do catch up with him?'

Hickory asked drily, 'What do you think we ought to do?'

'He's entitled to a trial.'

Hickory said, 'A trial like he gave Jerrold and Cheever and Erdman?' He immediately realized that he was playing into the newspaperman's hands by intimating he would not bring the Indian in alive. If they did happen to catch him and if he was killed, Logan would accuse him of deliberately murdering the Indian. Probably in print. He said, 'I'm sworn to uphold the law and I'll do the best I can to catch the Indian alive. But it's not likely he'll let himself be taken and you know it.'

'But you will try?'

'Of course I will. I think the Indian's misguided and I know he's killing the wrong people, but I can understand how he feels.'

They finished eating. Logan went upstairs to his room. He reappeared a few moments later, carrying a notebook. He sat down next to Mrs Dobbs in the boardinghouse parlor and began talking to her. Occasionally he wrote something in his notebook.

Hickory could see him from where he sat lingering over a last cup of coffee in the dining room. Lila sat down next to him and wiped her forehead with the back of her hand. Hickory said softly, 'The damn fool.'

'Mr Logan?'

'Uh huh. People aren't keen about having him write this story in the newspaper anyway. He'll just stir them up more going around asking questions and writing their answers down. Somebody might take a notion of knocking his damn head off.'

Lila didn't answer. He looked at her. She was tired and hot from the boardinghouse kitchen but the weariness in her eyes was more than that. Fear had taken its toll. She asked, 'How long is it going to last? And who's going to die tonight?'

Hickory shook his head. 'I don't know. I wish you and Jess had left on the stage today.'

Some people came into the dining room. She gave him a wan smile and got up to take their order. Hickory finished the last of his coffee, lighted a cigar, and got to his feet. Logan was no longer talking to Mrs Dobbs. He wasn't in the boardinghouse parlor at all. He had probably gone next door to the saloon.

Hickory went out onto the veranda and stood there in the cool night air. He had a feeling the Indian was watching him. And he wondered what kind of devilry the Indian had planned for tonight.

With people as scared as they were, it wasn't likely the Indian would be able to get any of them off alone. Unless he did something guaranteed to get them away from the safety of the saloon and boardinghouse. That meant another fire, Hickory supposed. And this time it would probably be the Dobbs house, the livery stable, or the boardinghouse itself.

He heard loud voices from the saloon, but tonight the doors were closed and he couldn't distinguish any words.

Suddenly the doors of the saloon banged open. A man came staggering out, propelled violently from behind. He stumbled and sprawled face-down in the dust of the street and behind him came a crowd of angry men.

Hickory recognized the man in the dust at once. It was Ezra Logan, the reporter, and he had been stripped of everything but his underwear. Before he could get up, he was seized by two men and held while a third man untied one of the horses from the rail.

Hickory hurried to the group. 'Hold on,' he yelled. 'What the hell do you think you're going to do?'

Marsh Haggerty seemed to be the one in charge. He said, 'We're runnin' the snoopy sonofabitch out of town, that's what. We burnt his damn notebook and now we're runnin' him out of town.'

Hickory said, 'So the Indian will do for you what you won't do for yourselves?'

Haggerty growled, 'Logan's the one that's feelin' so damn sorry for the Indian. Let's see how sorry he is for him when the Indian slips his knife betwixt his ribs.'

Hickory said, 'Let him go.'

'You go to hell! Put him up on the horse,

122

boys. Then give him a cut acrost the rump.'

The two tried to hoist the kicking, struggling, underwear-clad newspaperman onto the nervous horse. The horse shied away and someone brought him back and tried to hold him still. Hickory repeated, 'Turn him loose.'

The pair struggling with Logan looked at Haggerty. Hickory stepped closer and when Haggerty started to reach for the gun he had taken to carrying since the Indian came, Hickory said, 'Don't be a bigger damn fool than you've already been. Unless you want to spend the night alone down in the jail.'

Haggerty let his hand fall away. The two men holding Logan released him. Hickory said, 'Somebody get his clothes.'

Nobody moved. Hickory said, 'All right, Logan, get 'em yourself.'

Logan went into the saloon. He came back out a few moments later, buttoning his shirt. Hickory said, 'Go on over to the boardinghouse. Go to your room and stay there or it's you that will be spending the night in jail.'

'On what charge?' Logan was white-faced and trembling.

Hickory stared angrily at him. He said softly, 'I've got trouble enough without arguing with you. Are you going to do what I told you to?'

Logan looked at his face. Then he turned

and scurried toward the boardinghouse. Hickory looked at Haggerty and the others disgustedly, 'Go on back inside. And start trying to act like you're more than ten years old.' He didn't wait to see if they complied. He headed for the boardinghouse, a little surprised that the Indian hadn't taken advantage of the milling crowd to make his kill.

CHAPTER FOURTEEN

There was a growing fatalism in Hickory. Tomorrow, when they went after the Indian, it was just going to be an exercise in futility. They'd pursue the Cheyenne until middle or late afternoon and then the savage's trail would turn back toward town. By the time they reached it, it would be dark and their chance of catching the Indian gone.

The way it had to end, and he admitted that now, was in a duel to the death between himself and the Indian. In darkness, alone, man against man. And he had an uneasy feeling that it would be the Indian who would win.

Overcome by gloomy foreboding, he went into the boardinghouse. Jess was still playing in a corner of the dining room. Lila was wiping the table and straightening the chairs. He said, 'When you get through, I want to talk to you.'

She glanced at him curiously, but she did not comment. She worked for another ten minutes, then took off her apron and came toward him. The dining room was deserted, as good a place to talk as could be found. Lila sat down in a chair and Hickory rearranged his own so that he was facing her.

He felt more nervous than when he had gone out into the darkness alone to face the Indian. He said, 'I'm a good bit older than you. Damn near old enough to be your pa.'

Her face was blank and her eyes watched him steadily. 'Yes, Hickory. You are.'

'You can say no if you want.'

'No to what?'

He thought there was a twinkle in her eyes, then decided that he had been wrong. He said, 'I ain't likely to ever be more than I am right now, and maybe I won't even have a job when this is over with.'

She said, 'Hickory, what are you trying to say?'

He was sure of the twinkle now. He said, 'Damn it, you know perfectly well what I'm trying to say. I want you to marry me. Maybe it ain't right, but we're both alone and Jess needs a man and I sure do need you.'

She said, 'Yes.'

Hickory asked, 'Yes what?'

'Yes, I'll marry you.'

He looked around at the door leading to the parlor. She was smiling now. 'We're alone.

125

You can kiss me, Hickory.'

He did, awkwardly because of the fact that they were both sitting down. She stood up, and so did he, and the second kiss was more satisfying. So much so that he nearly broke her ribs.

Jess was watching, wide-eyed, from the corner of the room. Lila said, 'Jess, come here.'

He came, timidly. She asked, 'How would you like it if Hickory lived with us?'

He looked at Hickory solemnly for a moment. Then he grinned. Hickory said, 'There's your answer.'

Lila asked, 'When?'

'When I get that damned Indian.' He realized suddenly that without the Indian he'd never have asked Lila to marry him. At least not for a long, long time. He heard a shout from outside and went quickly to the window of the dining room. He pulled aside the blind and looked.

There was a red glow in the sky and it was coming from Chris Dobbs's house. The fire had apparently been started against the rear wall of the house, or inside, and it had not been seen until it had a start.

He said, 'I've got to go. Stay inside and keep Jess with you.'

He didn't wait for her reply. He ran through the boardinghouse parlor and out into the street. Almost everybody in town had gathered there. They were staring toward the fire, which

126

was mounting rapidly. It gave off sounds like a series of pistol shots in addition to a steady roar. Chris Dobbs yelled, 'Somebody help! We can put it out if we all work at it!'

Nobody moved. Chris bawled, 'For God's sake, help! It's everything we got! Won't nobody help?'

Still nobody moved. Chris began to run toward the burning house. Hickory shouted at him but he paid no attention. Hickory turned to face the gathering townspeople. 'Hasn't Chris got any friends?'

Four men came shuffling reluctantly forward. Hickory yelled, 'All right then, go help him out! I'll come along and keep an eye on you!'

He had snatched up his rifle as he left the boardinghouse. Now, carrying it, he followed the four men across the street and through the vacant lot toward Chris Dobbs's big house. He could see it was useless, but he hadn't been able to stop Dobbs and he knew if someone didn't go over and protect Dobbs the Indian would kill him. That was why the Indian had set the fire, to draw somebody out. He might already have killed Dobbs for all he knew.

With relief, he glimpsed Dobbs rounding the corner of the house. The four men ran ahead and Hickory kept glancing to right and left, looking for the Cheyenne. He wouldn't attack five of them. He'd try for Dobbs, or he'd wait until one man got separated from the others,

127

practically a certainty if they were going to try putting the fire out.

Hickory and the four with him could see even before they glimpsed the rear of the house that it was no use. A hundred men with buckets couldn't put this fire out or even stop it from consuming the rest of the house. It had too good a start.

Dobbs had disappeared. Into the house, Hickory supposed. The man had probably gone inside to save something he valued and had forgotten earlier. Hickory stopped running. The others did too. The heat was intense even from fifty feet away. The flames lighted an area two or three hundred yards away from it.

Hickory didn't see how anybody could have gone into that house and survived. He yelled, 'A couple of you go around in front in case he comes out that way!'

Two of the men left. Hickory yelled after them, 'Stay together, and keep your eyes open. You can bet that sonofabitch is around someplace!'

Around someplace. With a rifle whose magazine was nearly full. He kept staring at the rear door of the house as the fire grew, and listening in case the men out front should yell that Dobbs had come safely out.

So far, the fire had spared the back door but that was about all it had spared. Hickory kept his eyes fixed on the door, waiting for Dobbs to emerge. The man was a fool, he thought. Nothing material was worth going into a holocaust like that. No material thing was worth giving up life and that was what Dobbs was going to do if he didn't come out soon. In five more minutes, the back door was going to be a sheet of flame and there would be no getting out. The inside of the kitchen must already be an oven and Dobbs might already be overcome by heat or smoke.

Hickory looked at the two men who had stayed with him. He couldn't order either of them into the house. He wouldn't have even if he could. He said, 'Stay here and keep your eyes open,' and ran for the back door. He dropped his rifle on the ground forty or fifty feet away and unbuckled his holster revolver and gunbelt and dropped them on the ground with the rifle. He didn't need cartridges going off from the heat. He'd have trouble enough as it was.

As he approached the burning back wall of the house, the heat became almost unendurable. He raised both arms, folding them in front of his face to shield it from the heat. He was a damned fool, he told himself. Nothing could be alive in there. Dobbs had sacrificed himself and he would be as big a fool if he sacrificed himself trying to bring the body out.

But he didn't stop. He reached the back door. He knew the knob would be hot, so he shoved open the door with his shoulder.

The kitchen was blue with smoke and he couldn't see across it despite the light of the flames. Smoke hit him in the face and heat singed his hair and seared his skin. He plunged across the room, knowing he'd never find Dobbs, knowing that Dobbs had to be dead. Nothing could live in here more than a minute or two.

Halfway across the room he tripped on something and sprawled headlong. And he discovered something that might save his life. There was air down next to the floor, air only lightly contaminated with smoke, cool enough to breathe.

Something had tripped him, something soft and yielding. It had to have been a body, had to have been Dobbs. The man hadn't even made it halfway across the room. Or else he'd been heading for the door and had been overcome before he could get to it.

Hickory turned around. It was a body all right, and it was Dobbs. There was too much smoke to see clearly and besides Hickory's eyes were streaming tears induced by the smoke. He went beyond Dobbs, then turned and got hold of his arm. Crablike, he dragged Dobbs across the floor to the door.

Fresh air was blowing in the door. It cleared the smoke away and Hickory was able to breathe once more without searing his lungs. He crawled through the doorway, then got to

130

his feet and dragged Dobbs away from the house as fast as he could.

He must have burned his face and hands because the heat of the fire, even at fifty feet, was almost unendurable. The two men he had left outside now came hurrying to help. Each took hold of one of Dobbs's arms and dragged him on. Hickory cleared his eyes of tears long enough to locate his guns. He snatched them up and stumbled after the other two.

They didn't stop until they were a full hundred feet away from the burning house. When they did, they stared in horror down at Dobbs.

The man was dead. Blood from a knife wound had drenched his shirtfront. A patch of his scalp was gone, raggedly and hastily taken. His hair was singed, as were his eyelashes and eyebrows. There were angry burns upon his face and hands.

Hickory turned his head and stared with eyes still streaming back at the blazing house. Briefly he wondered if the Indian was still inside. For an instant hope surged in him, hope that the Cheyenne might also have been killed by the flames.

Then hope died as quickly as it had been born. The Indian had seen them coming. He had waited inside for Dobbs. He had killed quickly and had left before Hickory and the others came around the house. He was gone and his victims now numbered four.

A place was smoldering on Hickory's pants leg. It burned and he slapped it until the embers died. He nodded at the two men bending over Dobbs. One was Pete Arvid, the other Harry Spence. He said, 'Carry him back to the boardinghouse.'

He didn't know who would make the coffins now. Maybe they'd have to bury Dobbs wrapped in blankets. He guessed it wouldn't matter. Certainly not to Dobbs.

If only the man hadn't lost his head. If only he hadn't run on ahead and plunged into the burning house. Hickory wondered what he'd been so damned anxious to save. Maybe he'd had some money hidden inside the house. That would explain his recklessness.

He followed the two carrying the limp body of Dobbs. His eyes were still streaming. He kept knuckling them as he walked, and, when they reached the front of the burning house, he called the other two. 'Come on. It's too late to save anything.'

They followed; halfway back to the boardinghouse the two carrying Dobbs tired and put him down. The other two stepped in and picked him up. The Indian hadn't shown himself. Likely he wouldn't, Hickory thought. Likely he wouldn't take the chance. He didn't have to take chances. All he had to do was wait and sooner or later he always caught someone alone.

They reached the street, crossed it and

climbed the steps to the porch of the boardinghouse. The people clustered there stared with white faces and shocked eyes. William Whatley asked, 'What happened, for heaven's sake?'

Hickory said, 'The Indian was waiting for him inside the house. By the time the rest of us came around the corner the Indian was gone.'

'And you went in after Dobbs?' Whatley was looking at Hickory's burns and at his singed hair and clothes.

Hickory didn't bother to reply. His burns were hurting and so were the knife slashes the Indian had put on him. His hand ached and sometimes his arm hurt too, although most of that pain was gone.

Mrs Dobbs followed her husband's body in, weeping hysterically. She looked back at Hickory as he came through the door. 'Why don't you do something?' she shrieked. 'Why don't you get that murdering devil? How many more of us are going to have to die before you do something?'

Hickory knew there was no use trying to explain. She wasn't in a mood to understand.

Hickory's own feelings had ranged from disgust at what the Indian had done to fear to reluctant understanding of the way the Indian felt.

But now he was getting mad.

133

CHAPTER FIFTEEN

Everybody had gathered in the parlor of the boardinghouse. Orange light from the blazing house came in the door and colored everything. Even the saloon had emptied. Marsh Haggerty and all the other men were here.

Dobbs had been carried to a sofa and covered with a blanket. Mrs Erdman said in her harsh, flat voice, 'She's right. I say if the sheriff can't do something then we ought to get ourselves someone who can.'

Hickory held back his reply. It would serve no purpose to get into an argument with two bereaved women. But Lila Anthony spoke up. She said angrily, 'Look at him. He's burned from going in that house after Mr Dobbs. He's cut from fighting with the Indian. How many of the rest of you have done as much?'

Marsh Haggerty said, 'It ain't a question of how much anybody does. It's a question of getting that murdering redskin before he kills us all.'

Hickory said, 'Everybody's here. Hold a town meeting and decide what you're going to do.'

Several people agreed that it would be a good idea. Mrs Jerrold said, 'Mr Whatley, why don't you take charge?'

Whatley got up. He walked across the big room to the door. He stared outside. Hickory could see past his shoulder. The Dobbs house was now completely ablaze and was shooting flames fifty feet into the air. Fortunately, the breeze was blowing from the town toward the burning house and the sparks all blew harmlessly out into the prairie beyond the town. But Hickory knew they couldn't count on that kind of luck every time something was burned. Sooner or later the breeze would be blowing toward other buildings and they'd all have to get out and fight to keep the entire town from being burned.

Whatley turned. He was big and strong and a little florid. There was a reflection of the orange glow upon his face but it wasn't enough to hide the paleness of his skin. There was fear in his eyes, fear he was having trouble keeping under control. After nervously clearing his throat and stepping to one side of the open door he said, 'All right. We'll have a town meeting and try to decide what we should do.'

Everybody was facing him. One of the smaller children was crying and its mother scolded, trying to quiet it. Whatley said, 'Let us begin with a prayer.'

Back in the crowd somebody muttered disgustedly, 'Oh, for Christ's sake,' but Whatley ignored it. He closed his eyes and raised his face toward heaven. He said, 'Lord, thou hast visited thy wrath upon us in the person of an Indian. He has killed and burned and we are sore afraid. Tell us what to do, Lord. Bless us, for we meant no wrong. Turn thy wrath away and let us live in peace.' The same one who had spoken before said, 'Get on with the meetin'.'

Whatley opened his eyes. He tried to look stern but he only succeeded in looking scared. He said, 'Does anybody have any suggestions?' Nobody spoke. Whatley said, 'Everybody's complaining that something isn't being done. All right then, somebody tell us what should be done.'

Hickory said, 'We brought saddle horses in from Cruthers' place this afternoon. Come first light, we're going after that Indian. Maybe we can run him down, but I've got a hunch his trail will double back in mid-afternoon so that we'll just get back to town after dark.'

Whatley said, 'Well, that is something to try anyway. Who will volunteer to go with Mr Marks?'

There was a silence, then several men spoke up. Hickory said, 'I don't need more than three.' He picked Olaf Cruthers, Max Kaminski, and Juan Garcia. He told them to meet him in the boardinghouse parlor before dawn.

Then Whatley looked at the crowd. 'What else can we do?'

Frank Feeley stood up. He looked scared but determined. He said, 'How the hell do we even know it's an Indian? All we got is the sheriff's word. I say that if Hickory Marks and somebody made a deal to get their hands on this whole damn town then this would be a hell of a fine way to get it done.'

Whatley looked shocked. 'You have no cause to make an accusation like that!'

'No cause? What about Jess Anthony? The Indian didn't hurt him none, did he? And ain't Hickory Marks sweet on Lila Anthony?'

Whatley glanced at Hickory, who was too surprised to be angry. 'What about it, Sheriff? How do you explain the Indian sparing Jess Anthony?'

Hickory shrugged. 'The redskin lost his own two kids. Maybe he just didn't want to kill another kid even if he was white.'

Feeley yelled, 'That ain't good enough.'

Hickory stared at him, his anger stirring now. He said, 'It'll have to be good enough. You stupid idiot, you saw what the Indian did to me. You think I cut myself?'

'Why not? Things like that have been done before.'

Hickory shook his head disgustedly. He said, 'I handed this badge over once. Next time I won't take it back. What I want from the people in this room right now is another vote. I want to know just which of you want me to stay on as sheriff and which of you want me to quit.'

He saw the newspaperman, Logan, behind the others. Logan hadn't opened his mouth and probably wouldn't. But he was listening and he'd remember what he heard and if he got back to Denver alive it would all be in the newspaper.

The trouble was that fear was now dictating both the words and the actions of the people of Yellowhorse. They had come up against something they couldn't cope with and they were looking around for someone to take the blame. Hickory was handy and so was the newspaperman.

Whatley said, 'All right, we'll take a vote.'

Hickory said, 'Wait a minute. I want everybody to understand that if they're likely to want me out before this is over with, they'd better vote to have me quit right now. I don't want to go through this rigmarole every day.'

Whatley said, 'You heard Mr Marks. Now then, how many favor having Mr Marks step down?'

A scattering of hands went up, among them Feeley's and his wife's. Whatley said. 'How many favor having him stay on?'

There was no doubt about the outcome of the vote. The hands raised this time outnumbered the others two or three to one.

Whatley glanced again at Hickory. 'Mr Marks, you said you didn't think pursuing the Indian tomorrow would work.'

'That's what I said.'

'Then what do you think might work?'

Hickory said, 'We might try going out after him right now. Three or four men, that have got sense enough to stay together and follow orders. We'll search the town for him. Maybe it won't work, but it's worth a try. Anything's worth a try.'

Whatley asked, 'Who will volunteer?'

There wasn't a sound in the room but the whimpering of a child. Hickory looked at Feeley. 'You sounded off about me being in cahoots with the Indian. You got the guts to do what I've been doing all along?'

'Wouldn't take any guts if that killer out there was a sidekick of yours.'

Hickory said, 'I take it your answer's no.'

Logan said, 'I'll go with you.'

Hickory nodded. 'I need two more.'

Feeley said grudgingly, 'All right.'

Hickory said, 'If I'm in cahoots with him, you won't have much chance of coming back.'

Mrs Feeley said, 'Frank, don't go. What if you're right?'

Feeley shook his head. 'I'll go.'

'Please, Frank. Please don't go.'

Marsh Haggerty said, 'I'll go.' He was looking at Logan. Hickory shook his head. 'Uh, huh. You stay here.'

'Why?'

Hickory said, 'Because I don't want you, that's why.' He didn't wait for Haggerty to reply. He said, 'One more.'

Olaf Cruthers said, 'I'll go.'

139

Hickory said, 'All right then, let's go. We'll slip out the back door. I want all four of us in touching distance all the time so he can't get one of us without the others knowing it. And no matter what happens, nobody is to go charging off into the darkness after him. Understood?'

The three nodded. Logan looked as if he already regretted his decision to go. Feeley watched Hickory distrustingly.

Hickory knew he was a fool for taking these three men out. Olaf Cruthers was the only one he could count on. The others might panic and bolt for the boardinghouse, and if they did, one or both of them were going to get killed. But he also knew he had to do something. The people of Yellowhorse couldn't stand any more of helplessly waiting, doing nothing.

He led the way to the back door of the boardinghouse, after asking Whatley to lock it after them. He stepped out of the door first, instantly feeling that strange chill come to his spine.

He stepped to one side of the door to allow the others to come out. The door closed behind him and he heard Whatley shoot the bolt. He whispered, 'No talking and no more noise than necessary. And stay together like I said.'

He led off across the back yard of the boardinghouse. They couldn't move quietly enough to keep the Indian from hearing them. What Hickory hoped was that maybe they could get close enough to hear the Indian after he heard them. Or that he would think it was only one man instead of four and launch an attack.

He reached the corner of the shed behind the boardinghouse and stopped. Logan was trembling noticeably. Feeley's breathing was rapid and shallow. Hickory peered around the corner into the alley.

The burning Dobbs house, though now almost consumed, still gave out a little light. Enough to see along the alleyway. It was empty.

Hickory led the way along the middle of it. He was hoping the Indian would be out in front of the boardinghouse. He was hoping they could circle and come up behind the livery barn and surprise the man sufficiently to make him give himself away.

A hundred yards away from the back door of the boardinghouse Hickory began to move more quickly and more freely. He reached the last building on the street and turned. The high grass and weeds rustled beneath his feet. The Dobbs house was now only a pile of glowing coals, hidden behind the livery stable so that it made no light here.

He crossed the street and went beyond, now turning back toward the corral at the rear of the livery barn. He moved swiftly, getting anxious. Getting the Indian to give himself away depended on surprising him. Stealth wasn't likely to surprise him but speed might. The other three men came close on his heels, Logan and Feeley nearly tripping over his feet, Cruthers bringing up the rear. Hickory was suddenly grateful that Cruthers was along. He was tough and able and he didn't scare easily.

He reached the empty corral at the rear of the livery barn and suddenly he saw the Indian's horse. He stopped and raised his rifle. If he could kill the Indian's horse, the man would be afoot when daylight came and they'd have a chance to run him down.

He tightened his finger on the trigger, but just as he did, Feeley stumbled against him from behind. The gun blasted, flame shooting out from the muzzle. Hickory cursed savagely and jacked another cartridge in.

A shadow leaped to the shadowy horse's back. Hickory fired again. Behind him and a little to one side, Cruthers also fired. Then both Indian and his horse were gone, and there remained only the drumming of the horse's hoofs upon the ground.

Feeley screeched excitedly, 'Why didn't you hit him? Why the hell didn't you hit him? I'll bet you missed on purpose, you sonofabitch!'

Hickory whirled around. He swung an angry fist and caught Feeley squarely in the mouth. The man went back, tripped and sat down hard. Hickory said savagely, 'I missed because you ran into me, you stupid bastard! If you hadn't, I'd have killed his horse and he'd have

142

been afoot!'

Feeley got up and for a moment Hickory thought he was going to make a fight of it. Then Feeley apparently changed his mind. He grumbled something Hickory couldn't hear. Logan said, 'He's right, Feeley. You ran into him and spoiled his aim.'

'Then why the hell didn't he hit the redskin the second time?'

Cruthers said, 'I missed him too. He and the horse were movin' fast and we missed, that's all. I don't remember you doin' any shootin, though.'

Hickory said disgustedly, 'Arguing won't help. Let's go on back.'

It had been dark but not so dark that he hadn't been able to see the way the Cheyenne had moved when he leaped to the back of his horse. He'd been hit before tonight at least twice and it was possible he had been hit again just now.

Only his savage thirst for revenge was keeping the Cheyenne going, but sooner or later even that wouldn't be enough. He was hurt and losing blood and eventually weakness would defeat even his iron will.

CHAPTER SIXTEEN

When they stepped into the boardinghouse parlor, everybody was looking toward them hopefully, having heard the shots. Whatley asked, 'What happened? Did you get him this time?'

He was looking at Hickory, but Hickory did not reply. Instead, he looked sourly at Feeley. 'You tell him, Frank. It was your party.'

Feeley said, 'We spotted him. The sheriff and Cruthers shot at him but both of them missed.'

Cruthers said, 'Oh no, by God. You ain't making it that easy for yourself. Hickory had a bead on the Indian's horse and would've got him except that Feeley here rammed into him from behind and spoiled his aim. When the Indian heard the shot he jumped on his pony and took off. Hickory and I both fired. I figure both of us missed by God, but if it hadn't been for old stupid there running into Hickory, the Indian would be afoot and we'd have got him come daylight.'

Whatley said, 'There's no use blaming each other.' He looked at Hickory. 'What's next?'

'Nothing until daylight. Then we'll see if we can pick up his trail. Maybe one of us nicked either him or his horse.'

He was tired and out-of-sorts and he hadn't

slept well lately. His eyes found Lila Anthony and Jess over against the far wall. It seemed to him that this had been going on for weeks. He raised his voice, 'We need two men to keep watch at the front and rear so the Indian don't try coming up onto the porches and getting in that way. Kaminski's going with me tomorrow and needs his sleep. So does Juan.'

He listened with only a part of his mind as Whatley selected two men to stay awake and watch. He didn't worry about relieving them. He figured the Indian was already gone, but even if he wasn't, he would be by midnight and then the guards could get some sleep.

He walked to where Lila was. 'I should've got his horse.'

'I don't see how you could, if Mr Feeley ran into you and spoiled your aim.'

He said, 'Nothing more is going to happen tonight. Go get some sleep. I'll likely be gone by the time you're up tomorrow.'

She stood on tiptoe and kissed him lightly. 'Be careful.'

He nodded. 'Not much danger out there in daylight tomorrow. Not much chance of running him down, either, but it's something to try.'

She nodded and took Jess by the hand. They went toward the stairs.

Hickory sank down onto the nearest sofa. He pulled off his boots, stretched out, put his hat over his face and closed his eyes. He was almost instantly asleep.

He had expected to awaken by himself but he must have been more tired than he realized. When he did wake, Cruthers was shaking him. 'Come on, Hickory. Let's go.'

Hickory sat up and reached for his boots. Garcia and Kaminski stood behind Cruthers. All of them were fully dressed and carried rifles. Cruthers had a gunny sack which Hickory supposed contained food.

He got his boots on, picked up his rifle, and settled his hat on his head. He followed Cruthers and the others out the door, rubbing his growth of whiskers ruefully.

The horses stood tied in front of the boardinghouse, protected by the wagons. Saddles were thrown over the rail and the saddle blankets draped over the tops of them. Hickory threw his blanket onto a strong-looking bay and followed it with the saddle. He drew the cinch tight, then replaced the halter the horse wore with his bridle. He mounted and headed across the street. He had a hunch the Indian had kept going last night and it would save a lot of time if they were able to pick up his trail over behind the livery barn.

It wasn't yet light enough to see the ground, so all four men sat their fidgeting horses waiting until it was. Finally Hickory spotted the trail of the Indian's running horse and followed it. It headed straight away from town, easily followed because the indentations of the

146

horse's hoofs were so deep. Not until he was a quarter mile away had the Indian slowed.

Cruthers asked. 'See any blood?'

Hickory shook his head. 'But that don't mean he wasn't hit.'

'The way that damn horse was runnin', I'd say we missed *him* clean.'

Hickory said, 'The Indian kept going and it was early when he left. Maybe the reason was that he was hit.'

'Or maybe he figured he'd done enough devilry for one night. He'd killed Dobbs and burned his house.'

There was no more talk after that. Straight as an arrow, the Indian's trail led east, deviating only enough to avoid an occasional deep wash or towering butte. Hickory held his horse to a steady trot and kept his eyes on the land ahead, watching for a tell-tale lift of dust that would betray the Indian's presence ahead of them.

Cruthers rode about half a length behind. The others straggled out still further back.

A couple of hours out of Yellowhorse, Hickory halted and swung to the ground. All the horses were sweaty and a short rest would do them good. Besides, he wanted to study the Indian's trail.

He hunkered down, fished a cigar out of his pocket and lighted it. With his eyes narrowed, he studied the tracks of the Indian's horse.

There were ways to tell the freshness of a

trail but they never could be absolutely accurate, especially when the ground was dry, and this ground was. But Hickory knew that this trail was a whole lot fresher than the seven or so hours old that it had been when they left Yellowhorse. He was trying to tell how much. Cruthers knelt half a dozen feet away, put a knee down on the ground and studied the trail himself. He said, 'We're gaining. Or else he stopped.'

Hickory said, 'He stopped. I found the place a few miles back. He must have slept a couple or three hours before he went on again. Even that damned Indian has got to sleep.'

'And his horse is tired from doing this last night.'

Hickory nodded. 'But not tired enough to let us make up four hours' time.'

'Then what's the use of going on?'

'None. Unless he stops. This is more to satisfy the people back in town than anything.'

He got to his feet. He was chewing the end of his cigar, a sure sign of nervousness. He'd never been one to do useless things for the sake of appearances and this exercise in futility irritated him. Frowning, he tried to think of something they might do that would give it at least a small chance of success.

He said, 'We know the bastard is going to turn either right or left in the middle of the afternoon. We know he's going back to Yellowhorse. By God, it looks like between the four of us, we ought to be able to outsmart an Indian!'

Cruthers said, 'I don't know how.'

'How far would he go, once he turns, before he heads back toward town again?'

'Far enough to keep from being seen.'

'How far would that be? Two miles? Three?'

'No more than five.'

'All right then. Juan, you and Kaminski stay on the sonofabitch's trail. Cruthers, you head south and I'll head north. We'll go about two or three miles and then find ourselves a spot on top of a hill. Maybe we won't spot him, but it's better than all four of us wasting our time following.'

Cruthers said, 'Might work.'

'All right then. Let's go.' He mounted his horse and headed north. Cruthers headed south. Garcia and Kaminski stayed with the Indian's trail heading east.

Hickory knew that splitting his force would make it easier for the Indian to set an ambush. He also knew how unlikely it was that the Indian would even try.

He finished his cigar and threw it away. Looking back, he couldn't see either Kaminski and Garcia, or Cruthers. He rode for what he judged was two miles. Then he began looking around for a high point of land. He wanted a place where he could conceal his horse as well as himself. He wanted a place with a clear view of the land to north and south and east.

149

He didn't find one immediately so he turned his horse toward town. He traveled several miles before he reached a bluff with the rimrock side toward town. It was a perfect spot. He could hide his horse below the rim where he could not be seen by anyone approaching from the east.

He circled the bluff and climbed its slope. Reaching the rimrock, he found a place where he could climb up, and here tied his horse to a clump of brush. He slid his rifle out of the boot and climbed out to the top. He found a depression and sat down in it, facing east.

He knew it would be a long wait so he made himself as comfortable as possible. He stared out, studying a semi-circle extending from north to east to south.

The hours passed. The sun climbed to its zenith. Hickory was sweating and a couple of flies buzzed persistently around his head. A lizard came to within six feet of him, saw him and fled in panic.

The sun started down toward the horizon in the west. Hickory guessed it must be two or two-thirty before he saw a tiny lift of dust almost due east of him.

Immediately his heart began to beat more rapidly. If that was the Indian, he had an excellent chance of getting him. He continued to study the tiny wisp of distant dust until it materialized into a horse and rider. Closer it came, heading straight toward the butte.

Less than half a mile away now. And recognizable finally as an Indian. The horse had no saddle but there was a bridle on his head. The Indian carried a rifle across his knee. He was naked except for breechclout and moccasins. A braid lay on either side of his head. He held his horse to a steady trot.

Hickory eased back toward the rim, staying low so that no movement would be visible to the Indian against the sky. Reaching it, he climbed quickly down and untied his horse. The Cheyenne had been heading around the north side of the bluff. Hickory mounted and headed that way, excitement high in him. He had a fresher horse than the Indian had. He could run him down if he didn't get him with the first couple of shots.

Waiting, he almost held his breath. The Indian did not appear. Had the man glimpsed him and shied away? Was he even now a mile away, riding as if the devil was in pursuit?

Hickory touched the sides of his horse with his heels. The animal moved forward.

Suddenly the Indian appeared. Hickory had hoped he would be close enough for a sure shot but he was not. The Indian had veered aside to avoid a deep wash and was at least six hundred yards away. Too far for shooting even had Hickory been on the ground and had a rest.

The Indian saw him at almost the same time he saw the Indian. He drummed heels against his horse's side and reined away. Hickory kicked his horse into a lope and then, with a cut of his rifle across the rump, into a dead run. The Indian was going to make a run for it in preference to fighting it out. And that, thought Hickory, was his mistake. The Indian's horse was far wearier than was his own.

Hickory's horse leaped a gully, catching him by surprise and nearly unseating him. After that, Hickory paid attention to what was ahead instead of concentrating all his attention exclusively on the Indian. He gained slowly. The distance was already less than five hundred yards.

The Indian beat his horse savagely across the rump with the barrel of his rifle. Briefly the horse ran faster. But his tiredness began to tell. Little by little he slowed and little by little Hickory began to gain again.

Exultation soared through his head. He was going to get the man! By God, he was going to get the man, alive if possible, dead if the Indian insisted on putting up a fight, which he probably would.

Four hundred yards and closing. And now Hickory could see the Indian looking almost frantically around for a place from which he could make a stand.

Hickory heard a sudden, loud barking sound. His memory told him what it was but he did not react quickly enough. Too late, he yanked back on his horse's reins.

The animal was already going down,

somersaulting forward. Hickory sailed over his head. He hit the ground rolling.

It had all happened too quickly for him to prevent it. He'd ridden into a prairie-dog village and his horse had put a leg into one of the holes. The horse was up now, carrying a broken front leg, hobbling around on the three that remained.

Hickory sat up, hat and rifle gone, and knuckled dirt out of his eyes. His shoulder felt like he had broken it. His knee was twisted and maybe dislocated. And the Indian was gone.

Hickory cursed long and bitterly. It seemed like even God was on the Cheyenne side. He had taken the Indian straight through the prairie-dog village without injury. He had dumped Hickory so that the Indian could get away.

He got painfully to his feet. He found his hat, picked it up, and crammed it angrily down onto his head. He picked up his rifle and regretfully shot the horse.

He removed his saddle, saddle blanket and bridle. Throwing the saddle onto his shoulder, he limped disgustedly back in the direction of the butte.

153

CHAPTER SEVENTEEN

Hickory knew he was stuck here in the middle of nowhere unless he could attract the attention of Kaminski and Garcia as they returned to town. It might be in late afternoon or around sundown. It might also be well after dark. But if he did not attract their attention, he would be left out here alone with no alternative but to walk back to town, which might take until noon tomorrow. By that time somebody else would probably be dead. More buildings would have been burned and he himself would be further discredited in the eyes of the townspeople.

But he still didn't know how he could have done anything differently. The Indian had come into sight over a quarter mile away. He'd had no choice but to try and run him down. He probably couldn't have seen the prairie-dog village even if he had been watching for it. Sagebrush had hidden it until he was right in the middle of it and then it had been too late. The Indian had just happened to be lucky. His horse had barreled through the thing without putting a leg into one of the treacherous holes.

Before Hickory was halfway to the butte, his saddle felt like it weighed a ton. It was awkward to carry, and its edges bit into his flesh. Grumbling and cursing under his breath

154

he went on and at last reached the slope leading up the side of the butte.

He stopped and sat down on his saddle. There was one crumpled cigar left in his pocket which, fortunately, had not been lost in the fall. He took it out and repaired it as best he could by licking it and pasting the wrapper back in place so that it would draw. Then he bit off the end and lighted it.

The worst was that he felt like such a fool. For the second time in less than twenty-four hours he'd had a chance at the Indian. The first time Feeley had spoiled his aim. The second time fate, or chance, or bad luck, had ruined a sure chance of overtaking the Indian.

Easy to blame somebody else, he thought. Easy to blame Feeley, and the prairie-dog village, but in the end the blame rested right on him. He was the sheriff. It was his job to catch the Cheyenne and he had failed. He now faced the chance that his failure would cost another life in town. He faced the possibility that the life lost might be that of Lila Anthony.

Thinking that made him almost frantic with anxiety. He hurried up the side of the bluff and arrived at the top soaked with sweat and breathing hoarsely and raggedly. He dumped the saddle and bridle on the ground, leaned his rifle against it, and stared out across the plain in the direction from which the Indian had come. Kaminski and Garcia wouldn't be coming yet but he didn't want to take even the smallest chance of missing them.

He saw nothing, no lift of dust, no movement even though he stared for more than five minutes. Satisfied that no one was coming, he began looking around for wood to burn. He'd have to have a fire to be sure of being seen, by daylight or by dark. Otherwise Kaminski and Garcia might pass him by, even if he had seen them, even if he waved and yelled.

Little grew on this bluff but sagebrush, and he knew how hard that was to burn. He wandered along the bluff almost to its end before he spotted the gaunt skeleton of what once had been a cedar tree. He scrambled down the rimrock, which here was fifteen feet high, and began breaking branches off the tree. He gathered a goodly pile and carried it along the foot of the rim to the place he had gone up before. He carried up half, then returned and carried up the other half. Afterward he returned to the cedar tree.

He finished breaking off the branches. He was able to knock over the trunk by moving it back and forth. He carried the remaining branches out on top, then returned for the trunk.

It must have weighed a hundred and fifty pounds. He dragged it along the foot of the rim, then climbed up and got his rope from his saddle. He went down, tied it to the cedar trunk, then climbed up again, holding to one end of the rope. He knew the wood he had wasn't much. He knew he might also need the trunk if it got dark before Garcia and Kaminski came.

By wrapping the rope end around his rump and laying back on it with all his weight and strength, he was able to raise the cedar trunk to the lip of the rim. Twice he dropped it, to have it crash to the bottom again. The third time he was able to roll it over the edge and out on top. Exhausted, he sank to the ground.

He rested until his knee and arms stopped trembling. Then he turned and stared out once more across the plain.

It stared back emptily. Hickory searched around, found the cigar butt, and lighted it. He put his back to his saddle and waited until his breathing had returned to normal again.

Having finished what little had been left of the cigar, he got out his pocket knife and began shaving a cedar branch. He built up a pile of shavings six or eight inches high, then began adding small twigs to the pile. He increased the size of the twigs until finally he had a fire laid that he knew would start instantly from the flame of a single match.

Again he turned and stared out across the plain. He tried to guess how long it would be before the pair showed up. He considered lighting the fire and trying to attract Cruthers' attention but discarded the idea. Cruthers wouldn't be looking in this direction and might miss the column of smoke entirely.

So he waited. What would the Indian do tonight, he asked himself. The two biggest houses in town had already been burned. Remaining was Lila Anthony's house, built of logs and therefore harder to set ablaze. Remaining also was the livery barn, the biggest building in town and directly across the street from the boardinghouse. The Indian would probably fire that.

And who would die tonight? Nobody would, he told himself, if he could get back to town in time, and if he could make them stay together in the boardinghouse and saloon no matter what might happen to draw them out.

And tomorrow? What might he do tomorrow to catch the Indian? Another chase like the one today wouldn't work because the Indian would be on guard.

He got up and paced back and forth, occasionally kicking out savagely at a rock. He had missed a good chance today and he might not get another one. The worst of it was, he was going to have to admit to everyone what had happened to him.

He sat down again and gloomily scanned the land to the north and east and south. The sun settled in the western sky.

Hickory waited impatiently until dusk, having seen nothing of Garcia and Kaminski. Hell, he thought, they might have given up already and headed back toward town. If they had, he was in for a damn long walk.

He got up and began to pace nervously back and forth. He didn't have too much wood. He didn't know how long he could make his fire last and he didn't want it to burn out before Garcia and Kaminski were close enough to see it. Neither did he want to risk letting them go by in the darkness before he lighted it.

So he waited until first dark and then touched a match to the pile of shavings. He stood in the fireglow, wishing he had a cigar, hungry and irritable. He had lost a good horse. He had made a fool of himself. Worse, he had lost a chance to catch or kill a savage, cold-blooded murderer who wasn't through killing and wouldn't be until everyone in Yellowhorse was dead.

He paced back and forth until he was tired. Then he sat down, getting up only often enough to replenish the fire with a stick or two of wood. The sticks seemed to burn with frightening rapidity and at last he was forced to lay the tree trunk on.

He laid it with its middle in the hot fire and it caught almost at once. He'd let it burn through, then put one end in and finally the other end. If he hadn't been found by then he'd just as well start walking toward Yellowhorse.

He caught himself muttering beneath his breath, cursing the Indian, cursing the prairie-dog village, cursing his horse for being stupid enough to put his foot into a hole. But mostly he cursed himself for being so damned inept so far. He'd always thought of himself as being fairly competent to cope with whatever situation he was thrust into. In this case he'd been far from competent. It seemed that everything favored the Indian.

The cedar trunk burned nearly through and he broke it, sending up a towering column of sparks. He threw one end on and watched it catch. Staring out into the darkness, he thought he heard something.

He listened intently, and finally heard it again. It was a man's shout and it had to be Garcia and Kaminski returning toward town.

Shortly thereafter he heard the sound of a horse's hoof dislodging a rock and shortly after that the jangle of a bit as a horse shook his head. It was the most wonderful sound he had ever heard in his life. Kaminski and Garcia rode up the side of the bluff and drew their horses to a halt within the ring of firelight. Kaminski asked, 'What the hell happened to you?'

'Horse stepped into a prairie-dog hole. I had to shoot the sonofabitch.'

'How'd that happen?'

'Chasin' the goddam Indian.'

'Get a shot at him?'

'Never got close enough. When I saw him he was near half a mile away. I got as close as a quarter mile. That's when I hit the dirt.'

'Shoot the horse?'

'Had to.'

'All right,' Kaminski said. 'Give Juan your saddle and you climb up in back of me.'

Hickory handed his saddle, blanket, and bridle up to Garcia, who settled it on the horse's rump behind him. The horse didn't like it much but Garcia held his head up and didn't give him a chance to buck. Kaminski gave Hickory a stirrup and he swung up behind the man. He didn't worry about leaving the fire. There was nothing up here to burn.

They went back down off the bluff the same way they had come up on account of the rimrock to the west. At a steady trot they lined out toward town.

Once Kaminski asked, 'Seen Cruthers?'

'Uh uh.'

'Good thing we came along.'

Hickory grunted sourly, but Kaminski wouldn't let it rest. He said, 'Damn long walk to town.'

Hickory grunted again. Kaminski asked, 'What you going to tell the folks?'

Hickory said sourly, 'The truth. It ain't my fault the horse stepped into a prairie-dog hole.'

They rode along in silence after that and Kaminski seemed to know he had prodded Hickory enough.

But Hickory hadn't stopped prodding himself. He'd used up every idea he had for catching the Indian. What it was going to boil down to was man-to-man out in the darkness away from the lights of the town. That was the way it had to end.

CHAPTER EIGHTEEN

Hickory saw the town of Yellowhorse long before they got to it. Something was burning, sending a column of flame and smoke a hundred feet into the air. While they were still half a mile away he decided it was the livery barn.

The Lord couldn't have been entirely on the side of the Indian because there was a breeze blowing from the boardinghouse toward the livery barn, enough to keep the sparks away. They rode into town, fighting their terrified horses to get them to the boardinghouse. The closest they could get was the lot next to the store where all the other horses were tied and under the guard of Frank Feeley and Harry Spence. The two, each carrying a shotgun, didn't ask if Hickory, Kaminski, and Garcia had seen the Indian. Because of the fire they knew they had not or at least that they hadn't gotten close enough to do any good. Neither did they ask what had happened to Hickory's horse and Hickory didn't volunteer the information. He would just as soon keep what had happened quiet as long as possible.

The three rounded the corner. The heat from

the burning stable was blistering the paint on the front wall of the boardinghouse. All the pails in the boardinghouse, the saloon, and the store next to it were there, filled with water, in case there would be a shift in the wind, but the people were staying inside because of the heat, and maybe because of their fear that the Indian was lurking around somewhere.

Hickory glanced at Lila Anthony's house as he went in. It was over a hundred yards from the livery barn and unless the direction of the wind changed it would be safe.

The first person he saw was Lila and it warmed him to see the look that was in her eyes. She plainly had been worrying about him all day and now was intensely relieved that he was safe.

Whatley didn't even wait for them to take off their hats before he boomed, 'See him?'

Kaminski gestured toward Hickory. 'He did.'

Cruthers, who had been in the dining room, came out. 'What happened?'

'Horse stepped in a prairie-dog hole,' said Hickory. 'Threw me over his head as he went down. Broke a leg and I had to shoot him.'

'Where were you two?' Whatley asked.

Hickory told what the plan had been, ending with building the fire and attracting the attention of Garcia and Kaminski, who had brought him back to town. He asked, 'Anything happen here besides the fire?'

Whatley shook his head. Ezra Logan edged close to Hickory and asked, 'Did you get a good look at him?'

'Not very. He was six hundred yards away when I first saw him and I never got closer than four.'

'What did he look like?'

'Like any Indian. Braids. Naked except for a clout and moccasins.'

'Young, old—what?'

'Young, I'd say, but it's hard to tell with an Indian and I wasn't close. I couldn't see any gray in his hair.'

He was tired and he didn't want to talk any more. He asked Lila, 'Have you eaten yet?'

She nodded. 'Jess was hungry. But we'll sit with you.'

He said, 'Give me a couple of minutes to go next door and get a drink. You can go in and order for me.'

She nodded and went into the dining room with Jess trotting at her heels. Hickory went out, wincing at the heat. He hurried next door to the saloon. Marsh Haggerty stood behind the bar and there were a couple of men standing in front of it.

Hickory ordered whisky and Haggerty brought him a bottle and a glass. He dumped it halfway full. He gulped it down. Haggerty was looking at him questioningly but he didn't feel like explanations now. He half-filled the glass a second time.

He ached all over from the fall. The bandages around his slashed ribs and chest had been pulled loose, breaking the scabs and causing the wounds to bleed again. His hand ached steadily, whether from infection or the fall he couldn't tell.

He knew that Lila's house would be next, for all the difficulty of firing it. And he only had one trick left up his sleeve. After that, it would have to be hand-to-hand between him and the Indian, a conflict he had a gloomy certainty he would lose.

He gulped the second drink and slid a quarter across the bar. He turned and went out and hurried back to the boardinghouse.

Lila was sitting at the long table with Jess. There was a steaming plate of stew across from her. Hickory sat down and began to eat. Lila said, 'You can't blame yourself. It's not your fault your horse stepped into a hole.'

'Maybe not, but it's my job to get that damn redskin and I haven't been able to do it.'

'At least nobody has been killed tonight.'

'The night isn't over yet'

'I don't think anybody is going to be killed.'

He grinned at her wearily. 'I sure hope not.' He finished eating and was suddenly conscious of how tired he was. He said, 'It's been a long three days.'

'You'll get him. Maybe tomorrow. Have you got any ideas?'

He did. The shotguns the men guarding the

horses had been carrying. He'd failed with the bear traps, but one of them *had* caught the Indian's horse. Why couldn't he set a trap with the two shotguns over at Lila's house?

It ought to work, he thought, but he wanted to consider it some more before he told anyone. He said, 'I've got an idea but I'm not sure it will work. I'll see tomorrow.'

She was disappointed that he wasn't going to talk with her a while and it showed. He slid a hand across the table and covered hers. He said, 'I'm a bust. But I'm plumb worn out.'

'I know. Try and get some sleep.'

He left money on the table for his meal and got up. He stretched out on a sofa in the parlor with Lila and Jess sitting across from him looking at a copy of *Leslie's Weekly* that had come in on the stage. He closed his eyes and that was all it took. When he awoke, the parlor was dark and Lila and Jess were gone.

He got up and went to the front window. He pulled the shade aside and peered out.

It was dark. The stable across the street was now only a pile of glowing coals, but even through the walls he could feel their heat. The inside of the boardinghouse parlor was stifling, and the heat was what had awakened him.

He opened the door and stepped outside. A breeze blew up the street but even with the breeze, heat radiating from the coals across the street made standing here unbearable.

Hickory supposed the Indian had already

gone. For tonight at least. He walked along the street, past the saloon and store to the wall where the horses had been tied. The horses were still there but Feeley and Spence were gone. Hickory supposed they had gone to bed.

The horses were quiet. Hickory returned to the boardinghouse, went in and laid down again. The clock on the wall said five minutes after three.

He dozed occasionally. When he was awake, he thought about the shotgun trap, and planned how it could be set. He could find some small pulleys. He could string two ropes from the corners of Lila's house to a stake in front of it. If the shotguns were mounted on the corners of the house and aimed at chest height along the ropes, then when anybody tripped one of the ropes the charge would catch him in the chest. The only way the Indian could miss getting killed was if he came in on his hands and knees and even then he'd probably catch a part of the spreading charge.

It might work. You could trap anything from a mouse to a bear and there was no reason why you couldn't trap a man. He'd get it all rigged up during daylight but he wouldn't load and cock the shotguns until dark. And after the charge was set, Lila would have to keep her eye on Jess every minute of the time so that the boy wouldn't spring the trap and be killed instead of the Indian.

Hickory thought about Lila for a while. She

167

wasn't going to like this idea of his. She wasn't going to like the idea of a lethal trap set at her house. She'd be remembering the way Jess had gone home the other night after his cast-iron train. What if he slipped away and went home for something else again?

Hickory didn't like to think of that possibility himself. He was genuinely fond of Jess, but aside from that he knew that if anything happened to Jess because of him, things would be over between Lila and himself.

Gray began to lighten the windows. Hickory heard the stairs creak. Glancing that way, he saw Ezra Logan, the *News* reporter coming down.

Logan said, 'Well, at least yesterday went by without anybody being killed.'

Hickory sat up. Logan pulled up a chair, sat down, and studied him. 'What do you plan to do now?'

'Try setting another trap.'

'What kind of trap?'

Hickory told him. Logan said, 'And if that doesn't work?'

'Then I go out after him myself.'

Hickory could tell that Logan was thinking about that. He was thinking that Hickory would come off second-best and get himself killed, and that if he did, Logan and everybody else in town would have no recourse but to sit here like a bunch of sheep waiting for the butcher to slaughter them. Logan, for the first time, was scared.

Hickory said, 'What about your newspaper story now?'

It was lighter in the boardinghouse parlor, light enough for Hickory to see the look of chagrin on Logan's face. Grinning ruefully, Logan said, 'The story is going to have a slightly different slant. I don't believe, as I did at first, that the people of Yellowhorse deserve what is happening to them. Their failure to act immediately to save those Indian children was bad, but it was understandable. If the territorial government didn't dispute that carnival man's ownership of the children, then it's understandable that the people here would not. And besides, Mrs Anthony *did* rescue the children and try to save their lives.'

'Have you told anybody that?'

Logan nodded. Still grinning in that rueful way he said, 'You've no idea how much telling them improved their attitude toward me.'

Hickory got up and opened the front door. It was still hot, but ashes had covered most of the coals across the street and the heat was not as intense as it had been before.

The sun had stained some high clouds pink and the breeze coming from the south was cool and fresh.

Hickory stared at Lila Anthony's house. On impulse, he walked across the street toward it. Logan kept pace with him.

At the corners of the house, the logs

169

protruded alternately and would make secure anchoring places for the two shotguns. And since the house had no back door, the Indian would have to enter from this side if he wanted to fire it.

Rigging the trap would be easy, but Hickory had the uneasy feeling that the Indian would probably discover it and avoid tripping it. If he did, Lila's house would be gone and he himself would be faced with a hand-to-hand encounter with the killer that had been stalking Yellowhorse. The thought made his chest suddenly feel empty and cold, and he admitted that he was more afraid than ever before in his life.

CHAPTER NINETEEN

This morning, Hickory ate a leisurely breakfast with Lila and Jess. He had already told the townspeople what he intended to do, and they had universally approved. He had selected Cruthers and Whatley to help him rig the trap, Cruthers because of his general competence, Whatley because he was the blacksmith and could supply whatever brackets and clamps might be required.

Lila watched him uneasily all through breakfast and finally voiced her doubt. 'Hickory, is it going to work?'

170

He grinned, and hoped his dread of a personal encounter with the Indian didn't show. Maybe the trap *would* work, he thought. Maybe he wouldn't have to meet the man in a fight to the death. He said, 'I hope so. I don't see why it shouldn't.'

'What if he sees the rope?'

'I'm going to try and prevent that by putting soot on it.'

She studied his face nervously. 'A week ago, I'd have said this kind of trap was barbaric.'

Hickory said, 'It is barbaric. But we're fighting for our lives.' He looked at Jess. 'You're going to have to keep him with you every minute after that trap is set. If he went back again to get some toy...'

Her face paled at the thought. She said firmly, 'He won't slip away from me. I'll make sure of it.'

Hickory finished his coffee and got up. 'I'll see you after a while.'

'Can't we come and watch?'

He shook his head. 'The Indian is probably miles away but on the chance he isn't, I don't want a crowd over by your house. If he saw it, he'd be sure to suspect something was wrong.'

She came out on the boardinghouse porch with him. Jess had his toy train. He began to play with it in the dust at the edge of the porch. Whatley and Cruthers followed Hickory to Lila's house, each carrying one of the shotguns Spence and Feeley had been using last night to guard the horses.

Hickory swept the horizon carefully with his glance. He didn't see anything nor had he expected to. He was just nervous, he told himself. This trap was a last resort and he desperately needed to have it work.

And he examined his own feelings with mild surprise. Never in his life before had he been so desperately afraid, which was not to say he had never been afraid. A man who is not afraid when he fights is either stupid or a fool and Hickory was neither one. But he was more afraid of the Indian than he had ever been of any other man.

He tried to rationalize his fear, tried to decide why he was so afraid. Because the Indian was a wraith, he decided. Because he hid himself in darkness and struck out of that darkness and because he thus always had the advantage of surprise. Not only that. The Indian was an exceptionally savage fighter, who fought from fierce hatred for all whites and particularly hatred for those here in Yellowhorse.

Whatley called him over to one corner of the house. He pointed to a log about chest height on a man. 'We can lay it here, and block the stock so that it will point at a diagonal.'

Hickory nodded. 'Go make whatever brackets you're going to need. I want them strong so that no matter how much force the Indian hits that rope with, he won't jar loose

172

the guns.'

Whatley nodded. He took the guns and headed for his blacksmith shop.

Hickory went back to Jerrold's store. Mrs Jerrold was working inside, sweeping vigorously, trying, he knew, to put her husband's absence out of her mind. He said, 'I'll need some rope, Mrs Jerrold.'

She took him to a counter in which a number of holes had been drilled. Out of them protruded the ends of various sizes of rope. The coils were under the counter and there were tacks in the counter top to measure off various distances. Hickory picked a quarter-inch hard rope that wouldn't stretch. He measured off a hundred and fifty feet. He paid for the rope and carried it outside. Across the street, the embers of the livery stable were still hot and still sent up thin plumes of smoke. Hickory found a charred timber and by rubbing the rope across it repeatedly, thoroughly blackened it. He carried the blackened rope to Lila Anthony's house.

Cruthers had obtained a steel crowbar about six feet long and a sledge for driving it into the hard-packed ground. The two men sat down in the sun to wait for Whatley. Cruthers offered Hickory a cigar, and both men lighted up.

Cruthers asked, 'Think this is going to work?'

Hickory shrugged. 'Ought to. Unless he rides in, but even if he does, the charge ought to get him in the leg.'

'What if it don't get him?'

'Then I'm out of ideas.' He wasn't, but there was no use talking about what he meant to do if the shotgun trap failed.

After an hour, Whatley returned, carrying both shotguns, some iron brackets, a small sledge, and some spikes. All three men went to one corner of the house and while Hickory held the shotgun, Whatley mounted the brackets. He was unusually silent and finally Hickory asked, 'Does doing this bother you?'

Whatley nodded. 'I'm supposed to be a man of God and here I am setting a fiendish trap for one of my fellow men.'

Hickory said, 'He's killed four times. He'll kill that many more unless he's stopped.'

'I know. But reasoning doesn't help my feeling that what we're doing is wrong.'

Hickory let it drop. Nothing he could say would ease Whatley's conscience. That was something the man would have to work out for himself.

The gun was finally mounted and Hickory went out to a point in front of the house from which he could look straight into its muzzle. He had to stoop slightly and knew the gun was aimed exactly right. While Whatley and Cruthers mounted the other one, he rigged two pulleys so that the rope tied to the trigger would be about eight inches off the ground. He let the rope out and, when Whatley and

Cruthers had finished mounting the other gun, rigged the rope to it similarly.

Now he found a position in front of the house from which he could look into the barrels of both guns and where both were exactly lined on him. Here he had Cruthers drive the crowbar for use as a stake, and when it was done, stretched the ropes out as tight as he could without tripping the hammers on the guns, and tied them solidly.

To check, he went back and cocked both guns. He discovered that it only took a slight pressure on the ropes to trip the guns. A dog could trip them, or a cat, though it was almost certain that a cat would see the rope and jump over it. Hickory said, 'Let's pass the word around that anybody with a dog should tie him or shut him up. We don't want this thing tripped accidentally. And anybody with kids is not to let them out of sight after it gets dark.'

There weren't any horses loose, and there were no cattle close to Yellowhorse. It was doubtful if the rope would be tripped by accident.

Hickory headed toward the jail. Cruthers followed, carrying the sledge. Whatley took his tools back to the blacksmith shop.

Hickory went in the jail and closed the door behind him. He was jumpy and nervous. Trying to calm himself, he began pacing back and forth. The bear traps had so enraged the Indian that he'd killed every horse in the livery stable corral. If this trap failed, if he was only hurt and not killed, he'd turn on the town like a wounded animal and with all the angry savagery of one.

But maybe it wouldn't fail. Maybe one of those charges of buckshot would tear that damned Indian's head off. Maybe it would drop him in his tracks and Yellowhorse's nightmare would be over with.

He sat down behind his desk. He got a cigar out of the drawer and lighted it. The room grew blue with smoke and Hickory realized he was puffing almost furiously. He grinned ruefully. He'd have to calm himself. If he was in this kind of nervous state tonight and had to go out after the Indian, he'd have a lot less chance of coming out of it alive than if he was calm.

Lila Anthony came in. She closed the door behind her and sat down across from his desk in a straight-backed chair. She looked at his face for a long time, her eyes soft, her mouth unsmiling. Finally she said, 'This is a last resort, isn't it?'

He started to lie, to evade, then changed his mind. He nodded.

'And what will you do if it fails?'

'Go out after him. It's all that will be left.'

'Can't you take some men with you?'

He shook his head. 'He won't attack several men that stay together. He'll wait to get someone off by himself. He's got all the time in the world.'

'And we don't.'

'Nope. Besides your house there are only two big buildings left, the store and the boardinghouse. If he succeeds in setting fire to either one, the fire will take both. And the townspeople will be out in the open without protection of any kind.'

'So it's got to be tonight?'

He nodded. 'If the trap fails, or if he's only wounded, he'll be even madder than he was when his horse got caught in that bear trap. I figure he'll pass your house up and set fire to either the store or the boardinghouse.'

She said, 'You ought to get some sleep if you're going to be up all night.'

He nodded. She went to the door and he followed her. He said, 'Tomorrow it will be over. Let's take a rig and drive up to Pueblo. We can be married there and we can take a week before getting back.'

'Mr Whatley won't like it.'

'He's not a regular preacher. I know he's married some folks but I don't know whether it's legal or not.'

She smiled. 'And you don't want to take any chances? I'll tell you something. Neither do I.' She kissed him and went out the door. Hickory closed it and crossed the room to the couch.

When he awoke, it was early dusk. He got up quickly and took several ten-gauge shotgun shells containing buckshot out of the drawer of his desk. He went out, locking the door, and hurried immediately to Lila Anthony's house. He stepped carefully over the ropes and sat down on the stoop to wait for dark.

It came slowly, it seemed, but as soon as it was too dark to see the corral behind the remains of the livery barn, he got up. He walked slowly and carefully, looking for the rope and knowing where it was, but touching it nevertheless before he spotted it. He stepped over it, went to the corner of the house, loaded and cocked the shotgun.

This time he took no chances, but went around the rear of the house and loaded and cocked the shotgun at the other corner of the house. Finished, he made a wide circle and headed for the boardinghouse.

Most of the townspeople were in the parlor of the boardinghouse. Half a dozen of them asked if he had set the trap and he said he had. A few asked how long he thought it would be, but he had no answer for them. He couldn't even be sure that Lila Anthony's house was the Indian's target for tonight. Maybe it was the boardinghouse. Or maybe it was the store.

On the chance that it might be, he sent armed men to the back doors of both boardinghouse and store with orders not to show themselves unless a fire was started. Mrs Cheever was serving dinner in the dining room but Hickory was too nervous to eat. He wanted a drink but he didn't want anything to dull his senses. So he paced nervously back and forth until finally

Whatley told him to stop.

Grinning, he did, and stood beside the front door, listening. He knew he didn't have to listen. A shotgun going off over at Lila's house would be heard in every part of town.

Suddenly it did go off. Hickory, unconsciously waiting for it, nevertheless jumped as if he himself had been shot. He yanked open the door and raced across the street.

He was preceded by two men who had been in the saloon. All he could see was their dark shapes and he couldn't tell who it was. He bawled, 'Wait! One of 'em is still set!'

They must have heard him but they didn't stop. Behind him, Hickory caught a flicker of light and knew somebody was coming with a lantern.

Suddenly the other gun went off with a roar that was deafening this close. Flame shot from the muzzle for more than a foot. A man howled with pain.

Hickory raced on. He knew there was a chance the Indian had not been killed. And if he was wounded, Hickory wanted him before he could get away.

CHAPTER TWENTY

Twenty-five feet from Lila Anthony's house, Hickory encountered something yielding and stumbled and fell. He recovered, reversed his position, rifle poised to strike. But it was not the Indian he had stumbled over but a white man, who had cried out in pain when Hickory's foot struck him. Hickory thought it was Kaminski, but in the darkness he could not be sure. He didn't wait to find out, but leaped to his feet, ready for the Indian, if he was only wounded, to attack.

Nothing happened, except that Kaminski's companion knelt at Kaminski's side and asked, 'Max, where did you get it?'

'Back. Jesus, it burns like fire.'

The man, whose voice Hickory recognized as that of Juan Garcia, said, 'Help me get him to the boardinghouse.'

Hickory paid no attention. He was searching the darkness with his glance, but he saw nothing—no lumped shape on the ground where the other trip rope was, no Indian waiting to attack. He cursed angrily to himself. Somehow, and he couldn't imagine how it had happened, the Indian had avoided getting shot.

Whatley, carrying a lighted lantern, and some others arrived. Garcia got a couple of them to help Kaminski back to the boardinghouse. Hickory took the lantern from Whatley and walked along the other rope, looking for spots of blood.

Inside the rope, between it and the house, he found where the Indian had fallen. There were scuffed marks in the dust and the imprint of hands that the Indian had thrown out in front of him to break his fall. And there were several small spots of blood.

Hickory breathed a long sigh of relief. At least the trap had not completely failed. The Indian had been hit. How badly it was difficult to tell. Buckshot entering didn't make much of a wound, at least not a wound that would bleed very much.

He had miscalculated, and he realized it now. He had failed when he set the traps, to allow for the forward motion of anyone who might trip over the ropes. The Indian had been moving fast and so had Kaminski, and the fact they had, had saved their lives even if it hadn't prevented entirely their getting hit.

Whatley, at Hickory's elbow, said, 'He got away, didn't he?'

'Yeah. You take everybody and get back to the boardinghouse. Keep the guards on the back doors of both buildings. Put guards at the front doors too. That redskin is hurt and he's mad as a teased rattlesnake. No telling what he'll do, but you can bet it will be something. Hurry up, now, before he gets over being surprised.'

'What are you going to do?'

'I'm going after him.'

'You can't. He'll...'

'Maybe he will get me. But I'm going to get him while he's doing it.'

Whatley hesitated and Hickory said impatiently, 'Go on! Move!'

Whatley mumbled, 'Good luck,' and hurried toward the boardinghouse, following those helping Kaminski, who was yelling every time his body twisted a certain way, and the others, who were following them. Hickory saw Lila Anthony standing on the porch of the boardinghouse, but he yanked his glance away immediately. He needed every bit of concentration he could muster or the Indian would attack, kill him, and get away again. He did hear a shout from the direction of the boardinghouse, but he couldn't understand the words and paid no attention to it.

With the disappearance of the lantern, the complete blackness of the night enveloped him. There was a thin overcast that hid the stars, but even behind the overcast they provided enough light to see the building silhouettes. Hickory stood motionless, rifle held in both hands so that he could either fire it or use it as a club. He listened intently, but he heard nothing but the soft sigh of the breeze and the rustling of the grass as it bent before the breeze.

Maybe, he thought, the Cheyenne was hurt

enough, and mad enough, to make him reckless about noise. It was certain that he knew Hickory was here. He'd have been watching from nearby and he wouldn't have missed the fact that Hickory had stayed. He'd be coming, maybe was coming now. Hickory couldn't help the small chill that made gooseflesh stand out on his arms and legs. He turned his head, slowly, listening.

From the direction of the boardinghouse, he heard the faintest scuffing sound. He whirled that way instantly, eyes straining to penetrate the darkness. He saw nothing and didn't dare to wait. He leaped to one side, careless now of the noise he made, knowing only that he had to immediately vacate his position if he wanted to live.

Just as he moved, he heard a rustling in the grass on the opposite side, a rustling not made by the breeze. For an instant he puzzled over it, even while he kept moving, and had about decided the sound was imagination or caused by something he had dislodged himself as he leaped aside. Then he knew the blood curdling truth. There were two here, one between him and the boardinghouse, the other between him and Lila Anthony's house.

It was a possibility he had never considered since the Indian's first attack, the possibility that there might be two of them. He'd never found more than one trail, had never seen more than one or encountered more than one. But that didn't mean there hadn't been more than one. They must simply have stayed apart.

He had a terrible, sinking feeling that everything was lost. He was going to die and worse, he would be unable to take more than one of the savages with him when he died. The other would remain, to continue terrorizing Yellowhorse until all the buildings had been burned, until all the people were dead or had somehow managed to escape.

He heard the scuffing sound again, and suddenly, from the direction of Lila's house heard both scuffing and the rustling of grass.

A body struck him, hard, and at the same instant a woman screamed. The scream seemed to be no more than half a dozen yards away and was piercing and terrified.

The sound froze the body of his attacker for an instant, froze it with surprise. Hickory brought his rifle up and, raising it, caught the Indian in the throat. The knife in the man's hand was deflected by the rising rifle, but it slipped down the barrel and slashed Hickory's hand so deeply and cruelly that he dropped that end of the rifle helplessly.

He knew immediately that the rifle was of no further use to him. He would need both hands to use it and he couldn't count on the cut and bleeding one. He dropped it and savagely brought up a knee and it caught the Indian in the groin, making him grunt involuntarily.

Hickory knew Lila had saved his life with

her sudden scream and hoped she wouldn't mix in any further but he knew he couldn't count on it. He'd just have to finish the Indian if he could before she got the chance. At least there weren't two Indians. What he'd thought was the second one had been Lila coming to join him from the boardinghouse.

He plunged forward, drawing his revolver as he did. He shoved it out in front of him, thumbed back the hammer and fired instantly. The Indian, hit, staggered back, but he recovered before he had taken more than a couple of steps and before Hickory could fire again, attacked, bent over and hurt, but not showing it in the swiftness with which he moved. His only weapon was a knife, but fired by his maniacal hatred, he seemed to have the strength of several men. The knife slashed, and slashed again, and Hickory, cut both times, backed away and fired a second time.

The bullet seemed to have no effect, though Hickory knew he could not have missed the Indian. It was eerie and weird, as if the Indian was not mortal but some wraith or ghost that was impervious to wounds inflicted by mortal man. Once more the Indian plunged toward him, but as Hickory backed away this time, he slammed into Lila, knocked her down, and then stumbled and fell over her.

She was now between the Indian and himself and the Indian didn't care who he killed. This time Hickory didn't use his gun. It had seemed to have no effect before. He clawed past Lila, sweeping her aside with a violent movement of his arm, rising, threw his body against the Indian.

It was too dark to see where the Indian's knife was, or even in which hand it was. Hickory was simply putting his body between Lila and the Indian. He felt the burning thrust of it into his thigh and then he had overpowered the Indian and thrown him back and he was on top and grappling for the knife with hands that were slick with blood.

Lila screamed again, this time screaming to those at the saloon and boardinghouse for help. Hickory heard running feet coming belatedly, and suddenly the Indian was no longer a coiled steel spring beneath him, but a limp and lifeless body.

He heard the excited voices of the townspeople and started to get up. Then he remembered how hard this Indian had clung to life and he put his hand on the Indian's chest to make sure he was still not alive and dangerous.

But there was no rise and fall to the Indian's chest. There was no heartbeat. The Indian was dead at last.

Hickory got painfully to his feet. He could feel blood running down his leg. It dripped from his hand into the dust at his feet.

Whatley had the lantern. He held it over the Cheyenne and stared down at him. He said in an awed voice, 'Lord have mercy! That man's got enough wounds in him to kill a dozen men. All those times Hickory was supposed to have missed, he was hitting him. The Indian just wouldn't quit.'

Hickory limped away. It was over and he was tired and weak. Lila appeared at his side and took his arm and steered him toward her house. 'You come in here.'

He went in and collapsed into a chair, trying to hold his hand so that he wouldn't drip blood on the floor. His head whirled.

But he watched her as she worked and he guessed that any man who could meet a young and savage Indian in mortal combat couldn't be too old for what he had in mind. Even if the woman was a few years younger than he was.

She caught him watching her and saw what was in his eyes and her color deepened and she said, 'There can't be too much wrong with you if you can look at me like that.' And she set to work, bandaging his wounds, while he looked down at her smooth and shining hair.

Lewis B. Patten wrote more than ninety Western novels in thirty years and three of them won Golden Spur Awards from the Western Writers of America and the author himself the Golden Saddleman Award. Indeed, this points up the most remarkable apsect of his work: not that there is so much of it, but that so much of it is excellent. Patten was born in Denver, Colorado, and served in the U.S. Navy 1933–1937. He was educated at the University of Denver, during the war years and became an auditor for the Colorado Department of Revenue during the 1940s. It was in this period that he began contributing significantly to Western pulp magazines, fiction that was from the beginning fresh and unique and revealed Patten's lifelong concern for the sociological and psychological affects of group psychology on the frontier. He became a professional writer at the time of his first novel, *Massacre at White River* (1952). The dominant theme in much of his fiction is the notion of justice, and its opposite, injustice. In his first novel it has to do with exploitation of the Ute Indians, but as he matured as a writer he explored this theme with significant and poignant detail in small towns throughout the early West. Crimes, such as rape or lynching, were often at the center of his stories. When the values embodied in these small towns are examined closely, they are found to be wanting. Conformity is always easier than taking a stand. Yet, in Patten's view of the American West, there is usually a man or a woman who refuses to conform. Among his finest titles, always a difficult choice, would be *A Killing at Kiowa* (1972), *Ride a Crooked Trail* (1976), and his many fine contributions to Doubleday's Double D series, including *Villa's Rifles* (1977) and *Death Rides a Black Horse* (1978).

We hope you have enjoyed this Large Print book. Other Chivers Press or G.K. Hall & Co. Large Print books are available at your library or directly from the publishers.

For more information about current and forthcoming titles, please call or write, without obligation, to:

Chivers Press Limited
Windsor Bridge Road
Bath BA2 3AX
England
Tel. (01225) 335336

OR

G.K. Hall & Co.
P.O. Box 159
Thorndike, Maine 04986
USA
Tel. (800) 223–2336

All our Large Print titles are designed for easy reading, and all our books are made to last.